I dedicate this book to „Yasmin Sautter", who showed me „Ceee", an aspect of myself that I had never seen or perceived before. Yes, it always had been there. Now I Ceee!

Thank you for your wonderful friendship Yasmin!

Your Energy is part of the Stories and I know you already know this.

A big thank you also goes to Otis Wilga Laurie and his mom Lisa Brown from Australia for helping me refine the book and adding some of their energy here and there.

I´d like to thank all people and friends who were involved as inspiring co-creators. Sometimes it´s just been a word that I picked up or a picture I saw that lead me to a funny idea for a new Story.

I am grateful to be here at this special time, walking the Earth with all of you.

Carsten Götz

AF192208

Herstellung und Verlag:
Books on Demand GmbH, Norderstedt
ISBN 978-3-8391-6706-9

Ceee the Contents

Ceee the Contents

Introduction

Where have you been so long? Ceee

First of all, let me tell you, the reader, that I honor you. I honor the path you take, the choices you make and the things and events in your life that you create. I "ceee" you, absolutely equal to myself and to all other Beings around us. I "ceee" that our hearts and the love that we are able to perceive are the most important things in our lives and I "ceee" that we are connected to everyone and beyond.

"Ceee" is me. "Ceee is you" as well. "Ceee" is an aspect filled with love and humor, something that in a way I seem to have lost for a couple of years, though it always has been in my life. At certain events or circumstances it showed up but sometimes life isn`t easy. I guess everybody has been through rough times, more or less. This is all part of our life, though I now "ceee" that we always have the ability to stay in the realm of love and humor no matter what. I learned that from the person I dedicate this book to. Now let me explain how "Ceee" became visible.

My first name is "Carsten" and so I often used the abbreviation "C..." when emailing. What I couldn´t see was that whenever I used that "C..." the energetic feeling of the message was quite humorous and lovely and so different than when I used my full name. Messages with my full spelled name seemed to be very mind oriented and yes, there are times when this is needed and appropriate. So to go one step further there is a difference between "C..." and "Ceee". Yasmin told me about that dormant aspect. "Ceee" sees and perceives human Beings and circumstances from the heart and with a sense of a witty humor. Remember, you have that aspect as well inside of you, just in case you forgot. "Ceee" is the romantic warrior, soft and strong all together.

"Ceee" has wisdom with a lot of respect but doesn't take itself too serious. I am thinking about the true respect that emerges gracefully for you and for other Beings, not the false "rEsPEct" that is based on might and fear. As you might ceee I wrote it a little different to show that it is twisted and manipulated in itself.

Writing to you, the Reader should carry at least a message of true respect, tolerance and appreciation even more a heartfelt love connection that we share for the time you read my words and hopefully beyond that time.

Now let's start and with that I'd like to take you on a little vacation into our imagination and fantasy. Thinking about it the first and most important message from my heart to yours is: have fun with my creations. I thank you.

Let us begin.

I remember it vividly. It was early in the year of 2007 when I was lying in bed. It was 10:30pm and I suddenly had this story come into my head. I got up and wrote it down, more asleep than awake - 6 pages, written in English, which was very unusual for me.

The next day I began to write my first book. I started off in English but in those days writing in that language was too difficult for me and so I switched to German after a while.

When I realized that in parts it was me that the Shoe Story was about, it hit me kind of hard. This, of course had happened years ago and during these 3 years I had changed a lot. Inside of me has always been this driving force to move on and the willingness to evolve.

Ask an Ostrich if he could move on with his head in the sand. So the first thing is daring to look back into the mirror upon oneself.

To me it is fascinating how the Stories I tell have changed over time. No wonder because creating Stories is no other than what a painting is for the artist. The style changes, the colors maybe as well and the focus tells a Story in its own unique way.

The new Shoes...

An old man walked into a shoe shop asking the vendor to bring him the best shoes he had.

"*Yes of course*", the vendor replied, "*I got brand new ones from Paris. The finest leather you can get. Just look at these!*" With these words he handed over them to the man.

"*Well, well, they are really nice!*" and so he slipped into the shoes.
"*How extraordinary, I even can't feel them! They are so light. I want them! How much do they cost?*"

"*Oh, *", says the vendor, "*for there is no amount of money equal for being courageous. I tell you what! You wear them one week and afterwards you'll pay for them. Do we have a Deal?*"
"*Deal!*", though he had in mind never to come back. Feeling excited about the idea and thinking he had got an excellent deal; he left the shop with positivity.

The next morning turned out to be a great and sunny day, just perfect to show everybody his brand new shoes. He dressed especially, put on the new shoes and left the house. What a day!

After a short time walking he saw a man sitting on the street begging for money. As he wanted to pass the poor man he was asked to give a few bucks.

"Get away you bastard! Don't you see that I am rich and you are poor? We don't belong together!"

Something strange happened. As the old man wanted to move forward an unseen force suddenly stopped him. It felt like something would hold him back. Not being able to move on he started to feel dizzy and an impact of a strange movement.

As he collected his senses again he saw an old man standing in front of him, and strangely enough he found himself, holding his hands outstretched, begging for money.

"What the...!" his mind started to work but then was stopped. All of a sudden he knew why he was sitting here. He had lost his work lately and his little daughter was ill. Having not enough, he needed the money to buy food for his family.

Having this experience he again felt the dizziness and the movement, finding himself back in front of the begging man. Shocked and nervous he went away, giving a strange look to the poor man.

"What has he done to me? It is not my problem, I am not him."

What a strange experience, he thought a little later when he had calmed again. He decided to take a cup of coffee in a restaurant.

"A cup of coffee!" he ordered roughly, not paying attention to the sad and empty look in the eyes of the woman. *"Oh, okay! I know these types of people, they are just lazy!"* he thought as the waitress slowly went away to fulfill his order. As she came back he said in an angry voice:*"Next time a bit faster...!"*

Whoosh! Again he felt dizzy and this strange movement. He closed his eyes for the dizziness hurt them. As he opened them again he saw an old man sitting at a table drinking a cup of coffee. His feet hurt for he had been working for hours without a rest. He thought about bills to pay and an ex-husband who had beaten him out of the house. He saw himself packing his bags, running away, hoping that in another city he would have more luck. He knew why he was sad and empty.
Again - the movement.
He was back, sitting at the coffee table staring into the eyes of the woman.

"What was that again??" he thought. *"I am getting crazy!"* wondering if he had gained anybody's attention.

Obviously not; his heart was beating very fast and he drank his coffee in a blink of an eye.
"I'd like to pay!" he uttered and left the restaurant quickly.

What a day!
"Well, it is not my problem! I am not her!!"

He went out of the restaurant, turned right and started to walk. When a little boy followed by a group of other screaming boys came running towards him. Though there was a distance between them they were pretty close to catching him. Not paying enough attention the little boy ran into the old man, stumbled and fell down.

"Can't you watch out?? You ruined my new shoes!!!" with that he looked into the eyes of the boy and suddenly was looking into an old man's eyes.
He was lying in front of an old man. His knees hurt and he was frightened that the other boys would soon enough get him and play their "I-am-stronger-than-you" game. He was also thinking about his parents, who sure enough, would do the same.

Again there was the shift. He was looking into young eyes again. The boy stood up very quickly and ran away followed by the yelling crowd.
"Well, it is not my problem. I am not him!" - But he was scared.

What a weird day. As fast as he could he walked home, hoping not to meet anyone else.
He walked up the stairs of his house and inside his place.

"Ah, finally home and safe!" he thought, looking to the left, seeing the mirror hanging on the wall. He caught his own eyes and immediately felt a strong pulling towards the mirror. Finding himself in the mirror, looking into his own hard eyes he suddenly knew why he was that way. He once experienced a hard time having no money. That made him avaricious and being the tightwad he was, he wanted to keep his money and stuff very badly.

Another picture appeared. He thought about the time where he worked and worked. Being unable to take a short break for his boss would instantly fire him if he did. He felt worn out and sad, taking his anger home to his wife who left him one day, not feeling loved enough by him.

The picture of the days as a young boy came up, having fun, but there were always the "taller ones" who chased him just for fun. That made him fearful and angry but it also made him feel powerless and tiny.

Looking in his eyes the walls start tumbling down the first time. He cried. Now he understood what the shoes wanted to tell him. With the promise never again to be indifferent he changed back into his body.

Maybe, sometimes in the beginning he wouldn't do it perfectly but he would try and start again if necessary. *"How miraculous they are!"* he thought looking at his shoes.

Sure enough, he went back to pay for the shoes. *"How do*

they fit?" the vendor asked with a smile.
"Well, first they hurt, for the truth sometimes hurts but after that they healed the world."

The more often I read this story the more I feel that I'd like to have those shoes. Wouldn't it be grand to understand each other like that? A bit challenging, I admit. I would definitely choose them but maybe it just needs awareness and an open compassionate heart to ceee us in others.

I honor that story in many ways. I never had in mind to write books but in that night something happened that changed my mind.

Droplets of Enlightenment

Once there was a tiny drop living in the grand Ocean. He was
so joyful. He knew that he was part of something really big.
He knew everything about the fish, about the life under
water, and yes, he knew everybody down there. He had
Billions of other tiny drop friends and they had a great life!

One day a fisherman took water from the Ocean and put it
into a bottle. He would be going to a very unusual place for a
fisherman - the desert.

Yes, you are right when you assume that our tiny drop was in
that bottle too. Here he was with all his fears. His mind went
wild, thinking about all the drama for he had just heard the
word "desert" which is, for a tiny drop of water pretty scary.

 In fact it is a threat to his life!

*"I will just disappear!!!!! I will be dead and I will suffer!!!
Ohhhh, great spirit of the Ocean, why are you doing this to
me???? Wasn't I always a good drop???? Aren't I part of
you??? Now I have lost everything, my friends, my home and I
am going to leave this world soon!!!"*

If our tiny drop could cry tears he probably would have done
it now.

So one day he found himself in the desert. Boy oh boy, it was hot! Tiny drop's fear was rising and not just that.

He forgot who he was. With every second of his tiny-drop-life he forgot the Ocean. He forgot who he was. He forgot that he had tiny-drop-ocean-friends, loving him and caring for him. Sad tiny drop and here he was, still in the bottle.

He looked to the reflection of himself, reflected from the inside of the bottle and all he could ceee was a tiny drop of water. To him it was nothing special.

"*Well,*" he thought, "*I see who I am. I am a tiny drop, and just that. There is no secret behind it. I see it and I choose to believe that. I am just a poor drop. I am soooo tiny!*"

With that he surrendered. He gave up.

What the tiny drop didn't know was that our fisherman was a wise man. He wanted to teach something very important to this tiny helpless drop. So when he opened the bottle and the drop came out in his greatest fear, the fisherman said:

"*Don't be afraid! You could be apart millions of millions of miles from your Source, yet you still have the attributes of it. Yes, tiny drop you are still part of the Ocean! You have just forgotten the power you have!*"

These were the last words the drop heard as a drop. He ascended and changed into something very light and floating. He was still scared but he knew that something important was on its way towards him. He could feel it!

He traveled with some of his friends, the wind, birds and clouds. There in the distance he could see something blue.

Wasn't there a whisper? Wasn't that cheerful? *"He is coming home!! !"*

"I know those voices!! I know them!!! "He could barely hold his joy back!!
With that he was released by the cloud – vessel he was traveling with. He was home, remembering now all his friends and all the power he has.

Could WE dare to ceee, standing in the desert, that we are more than just a tiny human? Ceee

Indeed, I AM more than that. The main thing I do often is to limit "even the maybe's" which inhibits the possibility to let something grand arise out of nowhere. Here I AM. I am willing to let go of this habit.

A Rabbits tale

As soon as "Hop" the rabbit could run, he had these wild dreams. Whenever he would talk to other rabbits about them they would turn away making those funny movements with their eyes. Usually they laughed about this little fellow with the crazy thoughts saying that he was just young and inexperienced. *"When he is an adult he will become normal!",* his mom said that in a fearful way. *"I hope so…!"*

Hop never thought about being crazy or insane. To him, life was just grand and a joyful experience of never-ending explorations without boundaries.

"I want to learn how to fly!" he one day said to his mom.

"My dear Hop", she answered, *"you are a Rabbit! A bird has wings, where are yours? You are born to run and to zigzag when somebody chases after you. This is your destiny."*

As mom saw the sad and disappointed look in his eyes and his long ears hanging down like a branch of a weeping willow her heart opened. "At least I should let him discover this on his own. Eventually he will ceee and learn the lesson." She thought.

"All right, Hop! If you want to learn that, you should go and ask someone who will know. There is an old Owl living in the woods, go find her and she will tell you what to do."

Hop was more than happy. He barely could hold his long rabbit feet still. They suddenly seem to have a life on their own. Like lightning in a rabbit costume he whooshed out of their rabbit burrow and just stopped to rest when his little rabbit tongue was hanging out of his mouth. Catching his breath he began to think about mom´s advice and the Owl in the woods.

"Hmmm, how could I find the old Owl? She might be dangerous and hungry? Maybe she loves to eat little Rabbits?" his thoughts went wild.

This adventure surely was not easy but who said that it would be? He thought about the adventures in ancient times and the people back then who just left home not knowing what they would experience in their future.

Having these thoughts alone is quite unusual for a Rabbit, I tell you.

Hop felt a bit like a hero. Yes, I will go find the Owl and with that he headed towards the dark wood.

The first Being that crossed on his way was a deer. "Excuse me deer, could you tell me where to find the old Owl of this wood?"

"Oh, that is too dangerous! I mean, nobody has actually seen her but it is being told that she comes like a shadow and could kill you in a fraction of a second."

Gulp! Hop got rabbit goose bumps, whatever they are.

"But you can find an Owl just at night! Every little child deer knows that!", and with that and the head and nose high in the sky the deer disappeared.

"Ok! So she is dangerous."

Hops heart skipped a few beats hearing that. "Well, then I come at night again. I want to ceee and I am prepared. If she tries to get me I will run as fast as my feet can."

With that he checked them, like an Athlete would do his sport shoes. Everything was okay.

At night, when everybody was sleeping, Hop went back to the dark wood. He heard sounds like he never had heard before. The wind blew and made the trees talk and move.

"What am I doing here…?" he thought. "I should have listened to mom and the deer.

Suddenly he saw a fast moving small shadow above him. His eyes and ears caught the shadow disappearing into blackness, followed by a dull tone and a raspy voice clamoring. "Who put this tree here? It wasn't here yesterday!"

Hop got curious and wanted to know who made such a buzz. He found old Owl wearing huge glasses, cursing at the trees while holding his head in his wing.

"Ouch! I've got a headache!!" the Owl mumbled.

"Hello Owl! I am Hop, could I ask you something?" and Hop took all his courage to step forward.

"Oh, how many of you rabbits are there? Don't do any harm to me. I am just an old Owl Grandma with little eye problems."

After a while she added :"When I was younger I could see everything at night but today…hmmmm."

"Grandma Owl. I would like to learn how to fly!"

21

Grandma Owl begun to laugh and her feathers shook and her eyeballs rolled around like marbles in those pocket games for children.

"Well, if you have wings, you have to use them like I do.", and she moved her wings up and down until her feet were in the air. That easy!

Hop thought about his long ears. Once he heard a story about "Dumbo" a flying Elephant, but that was just a myth.

He moved his ears trying to use them like wings and you are right thinking that nothing happened.

 "You are funny, Rabbit! Who needs a flying rabbit in the air anyway? But I will help you."

There is a Tortoise living at the lake. She is the oldest and wisest creature living in this area. Go ask her and if she doesn't know the answer, forget your crazy idea."

Hop was happy. A small hint towards his goal was better than nothing.

"Thank you, Grandma Owl!" and with that he turned around heading home. "Go find your wings! I better walk home. That is much safer. These trees are a threat…." and he still could hear the rasping sound of her voice while veering away.

The next day Hop visited the lake. It was a beautiful spot in mother nature´s arms and it was a sunny bright day. Hop was enthusiastic to find another piece of his puzzle.

He found the Tortoise easily. She was swimming in the lake and looked more like an island than an animal.

"Good morning dear rabbit!" she sung with a voice like an opera diva. "Wow! I never expected something like that! It seems that some Beings have surprising abilities that one doesn't expect at first sight.

"Hi Tortoise, could you come out of the water so I could talk to you for a moment?"

"Of course I will!" the melodic answer came back. Singing the "Do Re Mi Fa So La Ti" all the time, she swam towards Hop.

"Just practicing, dear!" she said.

"Could you tell me how to fly?" Hop just threw the question out. "Hmmm, a Rabbit wants to fly. Now THAT is interesting! Why do you want to do that?"

"I'd like to ceee more. I wonder how the forest looks from up there. I dreamed about it and I can't get it out of my head."

"It's good that you follow your own dreams, Hop. I can help you but this may be a dangerous path."

Hop was excited. "I will do everything to make my dream come true."

"Okay, then follow the path to the hill on the other side of the forest. There, you will find something important but be careful."

"Thank you, Tortoise. Nice voice by the way!"

"It was nice meeting you dear! Yes, once I tried to sing in the Swan Lake but I didn't fit into a Swan's costume. Philistines!"

Now Hop's feet went to work. Like a rocket he whizzed up through the forest and up to the top of the hill.

What he saw made his eyes widen brightly. He smiled.

He saw a huge colorful Hot Air Balloon and Beings climbing into something that looked like woven reed from the swamp. After a while the Balloon ascended with a hissing tone slowly into the air.

"It is possible!" he thought. That was the teaching he had just learned. However crazy, follow your dreams.

I am leaving it up to your imagination, whether the very gifted rabbit has run home and worked in mum's garage, constructing himself such a Balloon. Showing his mom and all the others that he in fact could fly. Extending limitation and breaking through boundaries. I bet his mom was quite proud while all the other animals would stand with their mouths wide open.

I choose to follow my dreams and go for it. I choose to explore. This is how I AM.

Just a little Reflection

"I am done!"

Fred seemed to be upset: "I'm going to quit!""

"I don't want to see frowning people anymore and I definitely don't want them to show me their scars and every tiny pimple."

"But look Fred, this is your purpose and it is what you are good at! You reflect others so they could ceee who they are."

This almost voiceless voice belonged to Lilly, a little something that always smelled really good.

She added: "I could tell you stories!" and if she'd have a mouth and eyes you could have seen her doing a funny face.

"Look at me." Fred wanted to sound really serious now. "Nobody actually ceees me for who I AM. I'd like to be acknowledged. I have the feeling that people just look at me or even stare right through me."

He carried on, ''A lot of people come and show me what they consider to be their worst parts. I instead try to be really kind and nice, doing my best to reflect their true beauty."

"Oh Fred, you are too hard on yourself. I never have seen anybody doing a better job." Lilly tried to comfort Fred.

"Before someone brought me here I worked in an Indian Ashram and I learned a lot while meditating there."

"YOU?" Fred chuckled inside. "Come on…!"

"Focus on YOUR inner Beauty instead of the outside world!" and Lilly tried to impress Fred with a very wise sounding colorful voice. "You are reflecting the Beauty of God. Every tiny bit of it. Every single shade. Black, White and everything in between. There is Beauty in all of the colors. I can ceee you sparkling in the sunlight! I love you!"

"Wow, Lilly, thank you for seeing me and loving me!!! Oh, listen. Someone is coming, let's get back to work!"

"Yes, Fred!" and Lilly, the little piece of wise pink soap threw a kiss to Fred, the Mirror. "I am grateful to be here with you."

Scars conversation

Well, imagine that: three Scars lived together on a human body and during special occasions they had something like a social gathering, I guess we'd call it the scars regulars table or club scars.

Here they would chat and talk about what was new in their world.

"Tell us your story, Cheeky!"

The two cheering at Cheeky were Nosey and Chinny. Chinny was the youngest in the row. He joined the others a few months ago and so he was eager to hear Cheeky's wise words.

"Well, as all Scars do at first, we think really hard how to make an impression that lasts a long time."

You could hear that Cheeky was a really experienced Scar.

"I observed and contemplated, sometimes I hesitated for the time was not right. But then….after years and years…!"

"Yes?!" Chinny sounded overexcited.

"I was asked to concentrate myself in a special moment in the life of the body of this Being we live on. It was planned long time ago to catch this exact, special moment! I put all my effort into it and focused on all the experiences I know, and then I made it!"

"We should be proud to be here! Woohooo!" Nosey piped up in his nasally tone.

"Yes, but instead, we are not wanted. Think about that: The body owner uses cream trying to make us disappear. We should go on Strike!"

"We want to be loved! We want to be loved! "

All three Scars chanted in excitement.

The whole body begun to vibrate now and all the cells of the body answered. "You are right!" and so all the cells started to join in.

Believe it or not, suddenly the whole body vibrated with one voice, singing: "We want to be loved! We want to be loved!"

The man, owning the body just had washed his hands with Lilly the soap looking in the mirror named Fred. It was the first time he realized that the Scars in his face made him look really interesting. In a way it added a special note of wisdom to it. He smiled at himself.

Maybe the man one day realizes that he healed himself in that very moment; with a little help from three Scars.

D-light

"D" had great dreams. She always thought about getting higher and higher to fulfill that inner longing that she had since she was very young.

"D" used to live downstairs, with a lot of good neighbors and friends but she didn't like it very much. She thought that life "up there" would be so much more fun and brighter than down in her space.

I think "D" herself sometimes couldn't ceee the beauty of the building like it was, because for that, a special key was required that she was about to discover.

"The outside world doesn't ceee my importance and that's my truth. I'm going to scale up the ladder and then I will be who I am supposed to be."

Her neighbors shook their heads. "D", you can only be who you are. There is no need to be something different! THAT is the truth!"

"No! There is something more and I am going to prove it."

"D" replied, a little bit in frustration and anger. "They just don't want me to be better or greater than they are." she thought.

"D" had the ability to float around in the air, like all of her neighbors. It was natural to all of them and so one day she packed her bag and disappeared from home.

All her neighbors were in great turmoil. "Without her, we won't be the same any longer. Where did she go?" But no one knew.

It felt a bit like surfing the air and "D" enjoyed the ride. She was excited about all the adventures to come. She could not help herself but sing out with her joy as loud as she could.

This time, "D" was heard.

It was a man, sitting in front of a piano. "Yes!!!!!" he said, "That's it!!", and then he wrote something down on a sheet of paper, something that "D" knew from somewhere.

"Hey good man, tell me why you are so excited with glee?", "D" asked.

"I am happy because with that last piece, I have just completed something that will captivate and free people's hearts. They will love and enjoy it and that makes me happy!" he said glowing.

"I heard this note, a "D", which I needed to bring this master piece together and to an end."

"Oh.   That was just me singing! I can't help it but when I feel happy, I have to do it! But I wish I could sing better, higher and more beautiful." and "D" lowered her head.

"D, without YOU my whole concert would fall to pieces. I need you the way you are because this is your purpose. Ceee, you have a certain flavor, something that makes you uniquely you. There is no one else that could fit this role better than you. So own who you are. Embrace who you are!"

With that the master started to play his concert on his piano. Every time he played the d-key our "D" sparkled like the sunshine. She never thought she could be part of something grand like that.

"D" happily returned home, living downstairs on her own line of the staff. From now on, whenever someone composes something and needs her voice she would leave home for that special moment, helping to birth a new master piece.

And so it is.

♬*♬ ， ， . • * ¨ * • ♬♪   ♬*♬ ， ， . • * ¨ * • ♬♪

An Ant´s story

"Enna" was an Ant living in a huge colony amongst millions of others. Everybody always seemed to be so extremely busy, running around with a certain this plan or that plan. To them it barely mattered what the plan was, as long as they had something to distract them.

Enna was not like that. Since childhood, she could ceee things that others could not. She could find the beauty in every little creation. That was her talent.

The other Ants usually didn't want to hear about that "crazy" stuff.

"We have better things to do than daydreaming! Go find something where you could be useful and of service."

Enna had heard that voice with its special accent so very often in her life that now she always rolled her eyes hearing it again. It was "Ique", an old Ant that had immigrated from Spain. "Yes, Ant Ique. I will do that!" and with that she left.

Today was a beautiful sunny day, so Ant Enna decided to walk up a huge tree. She wanted to have a really good view over the forest that she and her colony lived in.

After a time of walking she was up high. Being able to ceee the blue sky with birds flying, she had a breathtaking view over thousands of other treetops.

"I wonder how many creatures live here, it must be millions alone, even in this small place!!", and with that she grabbed her little red and white bag, opened it and took out some fresh green pieces of a leaf.

"Pssssst!"

Enna turned her head. No one was there so she thought it must have been the wind.

"Pssssssssst….Hey you!" there it was again.

Enna looked around trying to find something unusual in her surrounding: "Who is there?"

"Can you ceee me?"

This voice was more like a fine whisper in her head than an actual noise outside.

"I´m here, just in front of you!"

In front of Ant Enna was a bloom coming from the tree. "Are you in the flower?"

"No, I AM the flower and I AM the tree also."

Though Enna had seen a lot of weird stuff in her life she doubted at first. "This is impossible, trees never spoke to me and I have been on that very tree so very often and I have never heard a single tone. Besides… trees can't talk!"

"You should believe your feelings and trust your intuition. That is why we never communicate with words, for words are so limiting. They can easily be misunderstood. A lot of Beings on this planet have lost the ability to really listen with their heart and their feelings! You Enna are a special Ant. We chose each other so that one day, at a very special time, you would be my voice in your world."

Enna almost chocked on the little piece of leaf she was chewing on.

"We chose each other...?" Enna frowned.

"Oh dear, you might have forgotten that, but the truth is the truth, even if you don´t believe it!"

"I am certainly going crazy! This leaf I am eating, that must be the reason!" Enna spat the rest of it out.

"From now on, we will walk with you and you can hear us everywhere. This is our first conscious gathering, the initial celebration of our re-connection. We will meet again soon!"

Enna was confused, oh you bet she was. Who would not be deeply disturbed at first, when ceeeing something like that for the first time. Ceeeing, yes, for ceeeing includes seeing, feeling and simply being.

Enna packed her ant bag and ran home as fast as she could. "I'll go to bed and tomorrow everything will be normal again!"

That night Enna had a strange dream. She visited the tree again, spoke to him, and laughed with him, cried with him and everything just felt simple, clear and normal. She woke up very calm. It felt like the wind had taken away her fear and blown it into nothingness.

"Good morning Enna!" she heard a voiceless voice.

"Was that you in my dream, tree?"

"Yes, we celebrated that we found each other again and you began to remember through your feelings."

"Great Spirit of the forest, Ceee me for what I am. I hear your voice. I honor who you are. Blessed are we for we are the manifestation of the Great Spirit of Consciousness."

Stone love

Once there was a huge and mighty mountain, looking over the land of the ancestors. Everything that had ever happened in front of his eyes he kept in his memories. He had felt the cold of the winter and the burning sun of the summer. He had seen warm nurturing rain in spring and he watched the snow crystals falling and dancing down from a cloud.

From time to time he had this wanderlust but this desire, he thought was something that with all of his power and might he never could satisfy. This longing to see the Ocean, or to feel the wind and its freedom to embrace everything, it laid heavy on his shoulders and his heart.

So every time a guest would come and was able and willing to hear his voice and breathe he would talk and ask about the world.

"Tell me, little bird, how is it to fly?"

The bird understood the language of his brother and so he sung in his most beautiful voice about it being wonderful to be free but he sometimes wishes to have more power.

A small cloud heard the beginning conversation and decided to stop and hold at the top of the mountain.

"Tell me, cloud, caressing my peak; have you ever seen the Ocean?"

"Oh yes, in fact, I directly came from it. It is huge, so huge that even you, little bird, with your wings couldn´t cross over. It is full of life, nurturing millions and millions of life forms. I have seen them, observed them, felt them; for once I was part of it."

"You were part of the Ocean?" the little bird wanted to know.

"Yes, I was. I ascended and transformed into this light reflection of myself. Mountain, if you want to experience the same, do like I did. Transform into something different and start your vacation!"

The mountain, standing strong and steady as he always did, started laughing. "You are funny and.... Crazy, little cloud! Look at me! I weigh millions of tons and can't move like I want. It's impossible!"

As little as the bird was, clever he turned out to be.

"Hey Mountain! Why don´t you send a piece of yourself out to explore? I am happy to help you with this for I could take a stone from your body in between my feet, fly up in the sky and you will start to ceee new things. After all it is part of you and contains your consciousness."

The cloud exhaled: "Hmmm, that sounds interesting!" and in doing so she sparkled in her excitement and shed a few raindrops here and there.

"How will I know, or ceee what my stone will experience?"

That was an important question from the mountain.

The bird seemingly had some enlightened food in the morning and so it was no wonder that he already had an answer at hand.

"No problem. At night, when you sleep you can connect to him and you will ceee through his eyes."

"Well then, little bird take this rolling stone here, he seemed to be perfect for that adventure." And the mountain pointed to a happy jumping stone that just fell off the top of his head.

The little stone made a funny face hearing that. "Are you guys stoned, or what?"

"I just fell a few inches down from the top and I am dizzy like being in a washing machine! Okay, I don't know what a washing machine is but, the point is, I can't do it! I am little; I am small, end of discussion!"

"Oh, come on, be a little adventurer. This should be a holy task to you, don't you think? You should be proud to be 'the one' that your daddy picked out of millions!"

The cloud was right. A few moments later the little stone found him being held by the bird's little claws.

"You better start now, before I reconsider my decision. Someone hand me over my pilot's goggles please and don't rock this little rock down here too much…!", and he jabbered a few more things that no one actually was interested in.

"Then, so be it! Your only task is to keep me informed about your experience!" and with that last sentence from the mountain, the little bird ascended into the sky.

Our mountain cried a few stones, waved his unseen hands with the invisible white cloth and hoped that at night he would hear from the little stone.

Higher and higher they ascended until Father Mountain vanished in the distance.

"Can't you fly straight?! I'm going to puke…!"

The bird was busy flying and holding the stone tight.

"Wow, this is getting heavy!!" The little bird thought after a while and a few moments later he said: "You might not like this, but….!"

And with that, he had no other choice than to open his claws, followed by a long descending "Ahhh!" from the stone.

Little bird put his wing to his forehead like he was a little bird soldier. "Sorry, but you will make it! Have a good time!"

Then he turned around, whistling the song "Papa was a Rolling Stone" and disappeared.

Meanwhile our little stone just knew one direction and that was basically down. Oh boy, that was fast like lightning. He closed his invisible eyes thinking that these were his last few minutes.

He entered the river with a more or less silent: "Plop!"

Suddenly he felt water all around but for the stone had never seen or felt water he of course didn't know that.

"I am dead! I am definitely not alive anymore!!!" he thought.

A pike saw the stone sinking down, thinking about a nice meal. Swallowing and spitting out again happened more or less in the same moment and the pike wasn't amused about that and bubbled: "You taste awful!!"

"What do you mean? I am stone on a secret and holy quest. "I am not your dinner!"

"What quest could that be, huh?"

41

If you ever saw a pike rolling his eyes then you are a rare individual, but in our story he did. The stone answered: "I am going to ceee the Ocean and I'm going to tell my father the mountain my adventures!"

"Then you are going to have a long vacation in front of you. This river leads into the Ocean, I know that. All you have to do is wait. Just head downstream and after some 20 years…!"

"20 years??" the stone uttered seemingly flabbergasted.

"Well, you are a stone, right? So time is not important to you! Bye - Bye! Have a good vacation!"

"Life is interesting!" and by just thinking about his father they were both consciously connected.

"Wow, I didn't expect it to be that easy!!" big daddy mountain spoke.

He listened to the little stone's tales, adventures and experiences. While emotionally crying a few more stones. Yes, it proves that a rough exterior sometimes hides a heart of gold.

From this day on the little stone and his father communicated every day, in fact, it was like the father could ceee through the stone's eyes.

Moments became hours. Hours, days, years and years went by.

The river did what he always did: streaming down. You never would find a river streaming upwards. That is what's called "the Flow".

"It is easy to travel like that! Life itself brings on the adventures and experiences and one day soon, I know it, I'm going to ceee the Ocean!"

Yes, the little stone travelled and with every more year rolling down the river he got rounder and smoother. With every moment he lost some of his edges in- and outside and some of his weight as well.

He crossed rough passages with white water and the traveling then was fast and easy. There were times where the great Mother Earth seemed to stand still and traveling in calm water took some time, year after year after year.

Snapshots of green forests, cities, fields became part of his and his father's experience and in a sense time itself became an observer of it.

Polished on the outside, smaller in his dimensions but wiser inside also, he finally found the Ocean.

The River released the Stone, smiling and happy to be part of the adventure.

Oh, what a joyous celebration that was!

"I made it! I really made it, Dad! I am at the finishing line!!"

Celebration.

There he was, on the ground of the Ocean, feeling the gentle waving, seeing fishes he never had seen in his life.

"Father is proud of me, I am sure!" with that he closed his eyes.

Again a lot of years past and even more years than it took traveling down the river.

For centuries he explored the Ocean and he forgot that his vacation didn't come to a complete circle. He still was in motion, like life always is. That is the purpose of life itself.

Starting his journey hundreds of years earlier in a far distant place, he one day found himself at a shore of a beach.

After all these years, the first time he felt the air again.

"Look at this shiny stone, mom!"

A young boy picked up our little stone from the sand.

"It looks so nice and colorful! May I take it home, it will bring good luck to us! Please?"

"You are right! You may take it home but treat it well and with respect."

Here we leave the little stone knowing that even at this point the adventure isn't over. Millions of these stones are on their way every day. Can you find one for yourself?

Life is everywhere and flows magically in every moment - even through a stone.

This story I dedicate to my habit of collecting stones when I am at a special place and feel like it. Some of these stones really magically came into my experience.

I remember walking uphill through a forest of a mountain in Tyrol, when suddenly I had this desire to pick up a stone.

I looked down and there he was. I liked it though I didn't pick him up. Too huge and way too heavy! End of the story.

Oh really?

No.

On my way back down, and I am talking about walking through a forest, crisscross with a dog pulling in front of me, I had the same desire to pick up a stone.

I was flabbergasted when I figured out that it was the same place and stone as before!! A really true story and yes, I certainly took him home!

I have another story about a stone and this story actually happened a few months ago, in early 2009.

I was doing some sports in a forest in the area where I live. Now and again, while I was running I had this desire to take a stone back home.

It was beginning of 2009 and the area was snow covered so I picked up a stone, looked at it but didn't like it very much. So I threw it away into the snow.

Funny that it hit another stone that literally jumped up out of the snow! Picking this stone up it appeared that this stone was heart shaped and you bet it. I took it home!

For today is the last day of the year, 31st of December 2009, you bet I take that as an opportunity to play with time.

So be my guest at a special party. The gathering of all the different times we have on Earth. Yes, for we have different time zones that describe the same exact moment on planet Earth, I give a few of them for now a personality.

The Gathering of the Time

It was a special moment, one tiny fraction in the endless row of infinity.

All the attendees of this great event, the celebration and birth of a New Year on planet Earth, were dressed up to the nines and waited outside the grand hall.

Everybody had the golden ticket, the invitation to this event and a must have to get in.

"Good Evening, have a wonderful time!" and the Chinese gatekeeper, laughing inside to himself for he found it very funny to say this sentence to time itself.

As always, someone is going to be the last and as the gatekeeper wanted to close the entrance door a younger time zone came running up the stairs to the entrance.

"Sorry, I am late! I am still not used to this Daylight Saving Time! I never know if it's one hour back or forward." and the gatekeeper had to really pull himself together not to start laughing out loud. "Sure, Sir, please have a wonderful…time!"

"This time zone really is behind the times!" he thought and then he closed the entrance doors.

Inside the party had just begun. Time zones from the whole wide world were there, each one dressed in a specific traditional suit or dress to represent the place of origin.

Music played and some time zones danced. Mr. UTC, formally known as Mr. GMT had fun with Misses Mountain Standard Time. The very correct Mr. MEZ from Europe shook his hips with the Atlantic Standard Time, though she wasn't really amused by his habit of stepping on her toes every while and then.

Champagne was served, someone toasted to this great invention – the invention of the time zone itself. Names were celebrated like the Italian mathematician *"Quirico Filopanti"* who had the first idea about a time zone system in his book *"Miranda!"* and the Canadian *"Sir Sandford Fleming"*, who was credited for his invention proposing worldwide standard time zones.

"It's been quite a story, how we came alive, don´t you think?"

Miss New Zealand Mean Time started a conversation with Mr. Moscow Time. He, to fit into the cliché, held a glass of the finest vodka in his hand.

"Do you know that every major city before that had its own time, just synchronized by the sun?"

"Oh, I didn´t know that! You are so smart!" and she gave him an admiring glance but then her attention fell on a young guy standing in front of a group holding up a glass of Champagne.

"Happy New Year!!!" he cheered to the crowd but in his glee he didn't notice that he was the only one raising his glass.

"Kia hari te tau hou!!"

48

„What is he saying? ", Mr. Moscow Time was not the only one with a confused look in his eyes.

"I guess it´s from the Maori language and it means Happy New Year! I don´t know though, I just had a few lessons in it." That was Miss Australian Central Standard Time who joined the conversation.

Mr. Moscow Time looked at his watch shaking his head. No, it´s way too early and it´s not even midnight!!

It was Mr. Kiribati Time, who was dancing and singing, cheering and swinging in front of all the others who watched silently.

"What's up? Happy…!" he wanted to start again.

A beautiful lady from the Samoa Islands raised her voice: ''You are far too early Mister, almost one full day!"

Now a bug tumult started. Everybody wanted to express that his time zone was the most important one.

"It is my time that is the right one! Your clocks are all ticking too slow or too fast!" and one time zone tried to be louder than the other one.

Like always, there comes a time when even the hardest discussion has an ending. Everybody tried to find his breath again.

The Chinese Gatekeeper appeared.

"Ladies and Gentleman, please give me your attention."

Everybody was exhausted and so there was not really a huge resistance to his wish.

"You are representations of a moment in space and so it depends on where you are to define your special New Year! Everyone of you is as important as the other one!"

Mr. Kiribati Time had a different opinion: "But I am the first one on the Planet so it is this exact moment that we change the year and everybody has to accept that! It can´t be that I AM in the year 2010 and the rest are still in 2009!"

"I ceee your dilemma, but where I come from….", and the Gatekeeper slowed down a bit, "the New Year is celebrated in spring which is in fact the southern hemisphere's summer."

Silence and for a moment time stood still.

"Well, if that is the case than it doesn't matter!"

Everybody raised a glass of something to drink and shouted: "Happy New Year, or not! It doesn't matter, the most important thing is to have a good time! "

Cheers – and a Happy New Year!!

TINIHANGA

"Meooow!"

The little tomcat turned around with a smile, presenting his little belly.

The wisest man in the clan frowned.

"Meoooooooow?"

"Oh, give him time." That was the little one's mom "Pai", which means "good".

"He is just a few days old, he will learn!"

"Matau", who was the wisest Tiger around looked at all the other Tigers that were standing around Pai and the little One.

Everybody wanted to see the new one, to tell all the others about him.

"We have to find a name for him but for now it is too early. We gather together again when the moon gets round three times. Then we will decide."

Everybody nodded and left the place.

Pai looked at her newborn who glanced at her with huge Tiger eyes. He was smiling like only a little tiger could.

"You will grow and learn. That is the circle of life."

Of course, the little one didn't understand what Pai was saying. He found it to be better to close his little eyes and fall asleep.

Pai herself closed her eyes, hoping that everything would turn out well. Matau never had waited to give a new born a name. He could ceee things that others of the clan couldn't and so it was a great mystery to Pai why he wanted to wait.

In fact, it was a mystery to everybody.

The Tigers on the Street started to gossip, that is always an easy choice when one can't say something interesting about oneself and wants to be heard.

Pehu, which means "loud", was good at this. "He is different, I tell you! He is not going to be a real Tiger! Did you hear what the others said…?" and she went on and on and on.

Yes, some Tigers are like that.

Sun and Moon danced in life's circle and the time went by.

No one knew that our little Tiger had a little visitor, he appeared to be a tiny flea, but inside he was at least as wise as Matau.

"Hey little One!", he one day started the communication. "I am Puruhi, but you can call me simple "Pu". From now on I will be with you until you don´t need me any longer."

The little Tiger first looked around trying to find somebody or something in his area. The wonderful thing with young Tigers and as well with young humans is that they can accept the unknown far more easily than older ones. Older Ones maybe would have doubted, questioned and maybe thought they were crazy.

Not so, the little One.

"Hi Pu, nice to meet you!" and magically and easily the friendship started.

Yes, this little Tiger was different. When his mom brought him a piece of meat he wouldn´t eat it. He once tried but disliked it. He thoroughly liked the green grass and the flowers, which is pretty unusual for a Tiger.

The others of course saw that and some shook their head, wondering with prejudice that his mom was not good or hard enough. Some Tigers preach acceptance and tolerance but find it extremely hard to be a standard for all the others.

So one day, when the full moon came back a third time, the great gathering started.

Matau looked at the little Tiger, lifted him up and turned him around and upside down. He looked at his paws and claws, behind the ears where Pu lived, into his eyes and then put him down again.

"Say Roaaaar!"

"Meoooowww!"

A murmur went through the hall.

"You are a Tiger! Say Roaaar and prove it!"

"Meoooow!"

"So be the name of this little One "Tinihanga", the Shape Shifter."

"I like that name", Pu said. "It has a hidden meaning! Good! All is well."

Pai his mom looked a bit sad. She imagined all the things the others would say or even think. The mind can be quick sometimes.

Tinihanga grew older. Yes, he watched other young Tigers how they fought against each other but he disliked it. He loved to watch insects, flowers, the nature in general and he learned a lot things about it from Pu his little body-buddy.

Time went by and sometimes the world is shaken, twisted and torn to be restructured again in a grander way.

There came a day when people told Tinihanga that his father "Ika" that means "Fighter", would be in town again.

Tinihanga had never seen him in and so he ran home as fast as he could.

Ika was proud. Ika was mighty. HE was a strong Tiger with a roaring "Roaaar" that no one would ever forget, even if a lucky one by chance did escape him, but that happened rarely.

Tinihanga ran around a corner and directly into Ika.

"Sooo! You must be Tinihanga, one of my....", and after a pause he went on to say "sons."

His voice sounded like thunder, deep, growling and frightening.

Ika looked at Tinihanga and in an impending sounding slow talking voice he added: "People say certain things about you. You don´t want to fight, you don´t want to eat meat and you sit and watch nature all day. Is that true?"

Tinihanga's world shattered. All he wanted was to be hugged, even without words, but what he got was the sense that no one found him good enough, not even his father.

Pu, the little flea spoke to Tinihanga. "Be honest with yourself. Your father can't ceee what I ceee. Stand tall and say yes!"

"Yes, it is true, father!" he said in a low voice.

"Well, I have an outstanding reputation of being the most fearless Tiger around so I demand the same from my sons. Something different is not acceptable for me. Either you change or I dismiss you as my son."

Ouch. That was more than painful. "You would dismiss me just because I am not like you?"

"My family always birthed kings and leaders. There is no space for weak creatures in my world."

Yes, this was the impression that Tinihanga had also. In this world all that counted was to be better, smarter, faster, and richer. There was no space for difference.

"I AM what I AM Dad! I can only be who I Am.", and Pu applauded with his tiny hands cheering a "Bravo!" to Tinihanga.

Tinihanga was sad. Though anybody with a heart would understand, He decided to go away from home to find a better place.

TINIHANGA

and Hinemoa

The forest was dark and filled with blood curdling sounds. Step by step Tinihanga and Pu entered it. He walked and walked endlessly, without thinking where he was going. Even the clouds in the sky seemed to cry.

At a river he stopped to drink some water. He stared at his own reflection, asking himself who he was.

"As a Tiger, who am I?" he said out loud.

"No time for an answer, right now I have a question for you. Do you know where I can find the Ocean?"

Tinihanga wondered why a stone could communicate and he was too surprised to give a quick answer. The river was flowing calm at the surface but quite fast at depth and so the stone moved very quickly downstream.

"It doesn´t matter!" he heard him yelling from far away. "I just let go!! Just let go! Just let go! JUST let go!!!!"

 "Just let go!" Pu repeated.

With that Tinihanga turned around in search of a place for the night.

Stars were telling stories and the moon mirrored the sun so no one would forget about her brightness.

"I am the Passionate Princess. They call me Hinemoa", he suddenly heard a voice in his dreams.

"I AM Hinemoa."

"Do not be afraid, Tinihanga. I am talking to you about Passion. For I once fell in love with a man from another tribe. His name was Tutanekai and nobody wanted him to be my man for he was not worthy in their eyes. To me, he was. So my passion brought me into his arms.

Tinihanga! Things are not like you perceive them. Be passionate about what you do and think. Be who you are from the fullest of your heart. Be passionate about the male Tiger inside of you and about the female Tiger also. Put them into balance; seek the Oneness to make them whole again."

"Be whole again!"

Tinihanga woke up from his dream with this beautiful Princess. He was so clear and real that he couldn't sleep any longer.

"Pu, did you ceee that too?"

Pu rubbing his eyes from sleep, answered with a yawn, "Yes, I knew she would come. Did you get the message?"

Tinihanga looked at the trees. "It was about being passionate about male and female aspects. Do you understand its meaning?"

Pu now was a bit more refreshed.

"Yes Tinihanga there are certain times when it is good to fight and there are certain times when it is good to ceee all the beauty in nature. There are certain times that need power and there are certain times when sensitivity is needed. Train both and integrate them well, but be always passionate and clear when using them. Sure, there are times when we don´t want to fight or stand tall but you will know what to do then."

"I understand! Hmmm… I feel soooo powerful. No one could ever stop me now… not even my fa…ther. Well… I guess he could, right, Pu?"

"Oh Tinihanga, don't start big like that! First start small. The time will make it work!" Maybe you could imagine Mr. New Zealand Mean Time smiling big hearing that.

The forest himself witnessed a Tiger growing up, shifting, balancing in and out, yin and yang, up and down, male and female, centering and becoming comfortable of where his consciousness rests. The flowers, while at certain quiet times were admired by him, could now ceee Tinihanga´s male aspects awoken. The "Meooow" changed to "Mearrrrooooo" and then to a very powerful "ROOOOAAAARRRR!" to then change back again to the cute "Meooow".

Pu was very proud of Tinihanga.

Years went by and Tinihanga grew up to a very strong but gentle and wise Tiger. There were some other Tigers that came into the forest to challenge him, for they had heard rumors about a very strong Tiger living there.

No one ever could beat him and so they all had to go back home, defeated by a mystery.

TINIHANGA

and Papatuanuku

One night a female goddess appeared in Tinihanga´s dreams.

"Don´t be afraid. I AM Papatuanuku, or "Papa". I reign over all animals, the forests and all that is between the Earth and the Sky".

Listen Tinihanga. I made you a special Tiger so you could lead the others over the mountain of uncertainties. Things will change in this area where your clan lives. All is good and appropriate, but your family clan needs you now and so I ask you to go back to them and lead them to some other place. This is my wish. This is why you grew up like you did."

Tinihanga awoke from this dream message, alerted and confused.

"I can't go back. They don't like me. They think I am a bad Tiger and not one of their species."

Pu, who was awake also now, heard that. With great wisdom and understanding he Gently said: "Forgiveness is a beautiful flower." and after a short pause he went on: "I ask you to pick a beautiful flower, make it a celebration for yourself. This flower of forgiveness is for you to let go of old sorrows, pains and your sad heart. Put all your attention into that flower and then let it go. Put it into the river and let it flow with the stream. Remember what the stone in the water said. To get to the place you want, you have to let go first. Otherwise the flows of life can´t pick you up and transport you there."

"How are you so wise, Pu?" Tinihanga asked.

"Well... Just like you, I had my dark times. Luckily I also had friends to help and guide me just as I have helped you."

Tinihanga picked a beautiful flower, similar to those a beautiful woman in the South Pacific would put in her hair. He then placed his attention on forgiving all that had been said or done by others or himself. He placed the Flower where it belonged, in the moment and let it drift until he could no longer see it from where he sat.

In one simple moment he healed himself and set free a power inside that he could never have Imagined.

"I have got to go back now and help my people." And with that he started his long journey back home, to where he came from.

Weeks passed and with each day and night the sun and the moon came for a visit. One fine day he stood on a rock overlooking the valley of his ancestors.

The clan of course already knew that an unknown Tiger had entered their land and so they sent out their bravest and most fearless offspring's to challenge him.

Every contestant came back, some had a black eye, some were limping but no one was ever killed.

"This Tiger is mighty! We never saw someone like him!" was the tenor of all who fought him.

Seeing that there was no other choice than to give in, Matau the wisest Tiger sent a reception committee and invited the unknown Tiger to speak and tell his demands.

No one ever had the slightest idea that it was Tinihanga, the one they had made fun of and the one that had been dismissed by his great father Ika.

He gladly agreed to the invitation and so he found himself standing in the middle of all the Tigers.

"Greetings wise Matau and greetings to all my friends. Listen closely, for I already have ceeen the signs in nature in this valley that something is about to change here. I have observed these signs since my childhood so I can fully trust them. This place isn't safe for you to live in any longer and so I ask you to let go of it and come with me to a place beyond the Mountain. I know that this is a hard decision to make, standing down and letting go of something big like this is a huge challenge. Look at the trees, they are dying. The birds no longer rest upon their limbs. See the water, it is stagnant and poisoned, it makes your beings ill. Can't you smell the Sulfur in the air?"

"We know how to fight, not to run away!" that was Ika. Tinihanga hesitated at first whether to go on but he remembered what *Papatuanuku* had shared with him.

"At certain times fighting hard with the wrong weapons leads us directly into a defeat. Think wisely before you use your claws."

Matau spoke: *"So be it. We will follow as you demand. You will lead our clan to a new place, for I also have ceeen the signs that you have spoken of but it has needed a real leader to guide us to a new place. I waited for you, Shape Shifter."*

Not everyone remembered Tinihanga or understood what Matau was talking about but they did as it was decided.

Tinihanga guided and directed his clan strong as a rock, showing Aroha, which means "unconditional love", to a new place beyond the Mountain. In fact the very same mountain that had longed to ceee the sea.

Tinihanga found a goddess in the form of a being. "Kura" was her name, meaning "Beautiful". They lived together and had their own family and babies. From time to time you would hear a certain voice that only Matau remembered and it goes like this: "Meoooow."

"Our cubs have their own journeys to make, their own mountains to climb and their own falls to heal from.

Our wisdom comes from understanding pain as something we can grow through.

The pain has an opposing energy, love.

Like a yin to a yang, none can exist without the other.

We can share this understanding through our actions and words. This is our wisdom!

We all share the same ability, to ceee...." O.W.L

The Glasswing

Everybody knows the Story about the Caterpillar, which transforms beautifully into a Butterfly. To us it is still a mystery and a grand metaphor for our own development.

So let us make this story about a brother and a sister named "Yan" and "Sim".

Yan was the older one of the two and the best brother Sim ever could imagine. They both were Butterflies and yes, they also know the Caterpillar story. They remembered how it was to crawl on a leaf, trying to find as much to eat as they could, just for the purpose of transformation.

The problem seemed to be that every Caterfly or Butterpillar left the memory of the transformation behind in the process and so in itself it was a mystery among all the Butterflies. Basically every group of Butterflies had their own beliefs on the mysterious events.

In fact some imaginative caterchild stories say that inside the cocoon the Caterpillar would melt to butter which congeals to form the Butterfly. Children talk like that, you know, easy.

The best Butterfly scientists were still trying to find out what actually happens but it was like digging in the dark, without any success. "We will invent even more powerful and sophisticated "Butterputer" and then we will hopefully know how to find a way to know, you know." That was a common phrase they used.

There also were the opponents of the Scientists saying that it was all conducted by a great presence that once died in spiders net. You could easily identify this group for their sign and symbol was a spider net to which they worshipped.

Some Butterflies were very sophisticated and lectured in secret Butterfly groups. "Butter and Bones" was one of them.

Some other winged ones said something like; the great "Butterlendar", a calendar found by an ancient Butterfly culture would actually run out of time in a few years, and I still can´t decide if it is sadder for the Butterlandar, the time that is running out or the Butterflies who believe in this, for their calendar will vanish eventually.

We also do not want to forget the great and long passed away Butterdamus, cousin and Butterfly counterpart of Nostradamus, who predicted the end of the Butterworld a few times, which actually never quite worked out well. His predictions though were always good to scare the above mentioned calendar group.

Then there were a few Butterflies that always talked about "Transformation". It was their most beloved word, yes indeed. These Butterflies were mostly considered by the others to be high in the sky. Common Butterflies often rolled with a few hundred of their eyes hearing stuff about it. The Butterflies in this group attended classes, gathered together, had fun and to some other Butterflies this was pretty scary.

"Crazy flies" was the term Butterflies on the street called them. Their ideas were sometimes too farfetched and sometimes too direct, for taking responsibility for own creations is always a huge step.

By the way: Any similarities to other species at this point are coincidental with all due respect.

Grownups talk like that.

Now we still have to tell a Story but all the things I mentioned above just shows the brilliance of diversity.

You will know in an instant to what group Yan belonged, for Yan always teased Sim that she would still smell like butter, sometimes behave like butter and would look like it.

Sim then teased him back, for Yan sometimes had a little problem seeing things clearly. "You're goggle-eyed!! Are you shortsighted or farsighted? Which one of your eyes is it anyway?! Are you cross-eyed?"

 To some other butterflies that sounded harsh but Yan and Sim knew that they loved each other beyond imagination. This love was simple but so real.

One fine day, when Yan and Sim sat in a Lilly slurping a glass of nectar, Sim had a question for Yan.

"You know, I heard all those stories about a coming of Transformation and everybody is talking about it. They often use our caterpillar-to-a-butterfly-stories to express that but what about us? I mean, we already are transformed, right?"

Yan, who had too big a sip of nectar, almost choked: "Yes, weren't those Caterpillar days great? Eating all the time Butter cream, crawling in the dirt…!"

"Oh come on, Yan! Stop teasing me for a minute and be serious. I mean, tell me, into which kind of Being do we transform from here? Do we have to go back in our chrysalis again?"

"And melt to Butter?"

Yan couldn´t resist saying that, but then he went on to say:

"Hmm, I heard about a kind of Butterfly that has wings that look like glass. This brother is called Glasswing and he looks so fragile that you actually never would consider him to be one of us. I believe that we will transform into Glasswing's."

Yan´s answer surprised Sim. Yes, she had heard about "Greta Oto" also but that also was a myth. She never had seen one with even one of her six-thousand eyes.

"Greta Oto" is a myth. He doesn´t exist!" she said.

Yan stood up, pushing the chair on which he sat with one of his six legs. "No! It is not. He is real and to become like him…"

"Yes?" Sim interrupted Yan, laughing because she never had seen him talking passionate like this.

"Breathe! We just have to breathe consciously, that is all?"

He now demonstrated the art of breathing but that looked kind of funny. Firstly, inhaling his proboscis looked rather snailish , then he extended his antenna and exhaled simultaneously, making a funny tooting sound.

Sim could not resist laughing. Haaaa.. hahaha…. Toooooot (as his own antenna shot back out).

"Don´t laugh at me!" and he ascended into the air.

"Come on. You are my best Butter-Brother, aren´t you?" Sim followed him still chuckling.

"But it´s true, and…." he sounded a bit ceremonial now.

"I now have a Kaupawah."

"You have what?" Sim shook her head so her antennas went from left to right and back.

"A Kaupawah, a Totem. I chose a human Being for that. Ancient Butterfly Cultures had it and now I have one also. He is assisting me and he is sitting right now on my shoulder. I can send him out into other dimensions and stuff like that."

"Oh Yan, you are going crazy! There is nobody sitting on your shoulder because you don't have a shoulder! You are a Butterfly!"

For a few moments their attention was caught by an exhausted looking, little, deep breathing blue bird with a stone in his claws.

"Too heavy, much too heavy, way too heavy…" and then he released it. Maybe you can ceee the mental constructions that fell down as well.

Yan didn´t give in. "Well, you don´t have to believe me if you don´t want to! I will have those fancy glass wings when you still have your old ones."

Now there was a pause in their communication. Yan obviously wasn't that childish at all and seemed to be very interested in expanding and developing himself to a grander Being.

"Okay, I will breath, I will choose a Kapau-whatever, what else can I do?"

Yan now started to sing and really expand his voice.

"Aaaaahhhhhhhhhhhhhhhhhhhhhhhhhhhhhhhh!", (I challenge you to ceee the little Butterfly with an open mouth trying to put as much power possible behind his voice.)

Sim now also started to sing and together they moved a lot of stuck energy for it is unbelievably liberating to express the voice like that.

At this point of the story a third butterfly joined them. First they couldn´t ceee him but when they did they almost fell from the sky.

It was "Greta Oto".

"Habla Espaniol"?

"What's he saying?" Sim uttered in awe.

Greta Oto spoke in broken English with a Spanish accent:

"I am sorry, I am From Panama. I heard about a cinema that shows a movie called "The Owl and the Bees" or something, a very famous story. Do you know the way?"

The "Happytrain"

Sam´s vacation had just started.

He didn´t expect it to happen that early but here he found himself, standing at a railway station in the middle of nowhere. Sam was an old man, though he was in pretty good shape and today he himself found even more so. He was dressed perfectly, like a gentleman. His white hair combined with his slightly brown taint gave him an interesting look and sometimes his friends teased him saying he looked like "Fred Astaire", though he never could dance like him.

The railway station where Sam was waiting for his train to come was filled up with a lot of busy and interesting looking people. The only thing he found a bit confusing was, that nobody actually carried around huge bags or suitcases. Sam dismissed his concerns thinking that there must be a good reason for that and he himself had also no need to have something to carry with him other than his happiness, love and peace.

Sam tried to find a clock but couldn´t find any and so he decided to go and ask the station master.

"Excuse me Sir! I can´t find any clock, do you know what time it is?"

The station master smiled at Sam, saying: ''Oh Sir, the train will be here in a few moments. Who would concern himself with the question of time if he is going on such a nice vacation! You, as our best customer deserve all the best luxury and comfort you desire. Would you like a coffee or a tea while you are waiting relaxed for the train?"

Sam was flabbergasted by the kindness he just experienced. He had travelled a lot during his life but there was nothing stranger than meeting a station master being that nice and inviting.

Sam gladly took a cup of tea and sat down close to the station masters office, who then glanced into the distance, saying: "Oh, here it comes." followed by an announcement over the station's loudspeakers: "Dear passengers. Please let first all the people get out of the train in their tempo and give all the arriving passengers' time to meet their friends, relatives or people who wait for them before you enter the train. Thank you for travelling with the Happytrain Line! Enjoy your vacation."

Sam watched the train entering the station, which was either the last or the first station of this track, depending in which direction you choose to look.

"Though,", Sam thought, "I prefer to look at it as always a beginning and not as an ending."

Passengers left the train, which was a very beautiful and romantic steam train. It was not like the ones that go hundreds of miles per hour, looking more like an arrow than the old trains. He liked the old look because it reminded him of a train that he had treasured in his mind when he was a kid.

"Everything today is about speed and being first, but today I simply choose to enjoy every bit of the ride without thinking about time!"

We switched location and moved to another railway station; in fact it was the same track just at the other beginning.

Here we meet "Sameena" a beautiful looking woman, who was also waiting for her train.

She knew where she wanted to go but nevertheless was a bit confused about it. Oh, don´t get me wrong, she was already at this destination place countless times, but it always was a different experience and turned out to be very surprising.

"I hope this time everything will turn out like I imagined and planned it. I am so nervous! What if the people I chose to stay with are unfriendly or treat me bad? This could happen! Hmmm, but what if I meet and experience real love? This also could happen!"

"Oh, don´t worry, Sameena! You will have a great experience, as always. Just don´t forget to send me a card, or talk to me and the most important thing is, don't forget me!"

This voice belonged to "Kiraan", her best friend.

"Look, you are not the only one who is jumping on this train. Just enjoy the ride and have a nice experience!"

The train entered the station. A rasping sounding loudspeaker that was sleeping awoke: "Dear passengers. Please let first all the people get out of the train in their tempo and give all the arriving passengers time to meet their friends, relatives or people who wait for them, before you enter the train. Enjoy the ride and thank you for travelling with the Happytrain Line!"

Sameena and Kiraan looked around watching the whole scenery. People left the train, looking around and almost everybody seemed to have someone to pick them up.

There were old people and young kids, people in their twenties and thirties, in fact, people of every age.

The few people who were looking around with nobody waiting for them were guided to the exit by employees of the Happytrain Line. It was a very nice and welcoming hello.

Sameena hugged Kiraan a last time.

"I'll ceee you soon!" and tears of joy run down her cheek.

"Be well!"

Sameena entered the train. Inside it looked beautiful and well designed. Everything seemed to be created with the mixture of real commitment, love and time. Questions like, how much something had cost? Or, does practicality mean nothing here? The purpose was enjoyment and expressing details in a most exquisite way.

"This is your seat!"

The smiling train conductress guided her to a cozy looking chair with a dark green cushion. Sameena handed her the ticket and everything was fine. "Refreshments are in the next cage, please be our guest and welcome aboard our Happytrain Line!"

The train filled up with a lot of interesting people and so Sameena found herself in a nice conversation with other guests about her hopes, dreams and her destination.

Sam also already had entered the train. It was the same type of train that Sameena enjoyed and Sam was flabbergasted by the beauty.

"Wow, that must have cost a lot of money!" he said to the train conductor, who just smiled and marked Sam´s ticket.

"You are a passenger of the Happytrain Line and so you deserve the best of the best. If you are happy then so we are. Refreshments are in the next carriage, please be our guest. Your seat is this one!"

Sam sat down and relaxed in the nice looking chair. The train filled up with other passengers, mostly older people but also a few younger ones.

Both trains, Sam´s and Sameena´s left their station.

Waving hands, a few tears good bye and fare ye well!

Sam was so relaxed that he couldn´t resist closing his eyes and falling into a light sleep. Meanwhile Sameena, after having an excited start, got calmer and more relaxed. She as well closed her eyes, dreaming and thinking about the things to come.

Sam opened his eyes, when he heard the conductor's voice.

"Passengers to the very Near Earth Realms please exit the train here. Our employees at the station will guide you to your next train which will bring you to your final destination. Thank you for travelling with the Happytrain Line!"

Sam never had heard of a city or town like this but obviously a lot had. It seemed they had no choice other than to exit the train here. Like attracts like and so it is the same with resonating frequencies.

"I'm going to see my son! He so needs me, you know! Never can do any step without me." An elderly looking woman was smiling in hope. This was her heaven.

A man in a grey suit answered: "Oh, I'm joining with my church friends! Looking forward to it and waited for that a long time, though it will be challenging first, I know. It's hard to be a son of god, you know. You always have to do the right thing so that he is happy with you."

Yes, this was the expression and his idea about heaven.

Another man, wearing a colorful shirt and short trousers with a glass of Whiskey in his hands started laughing hearing that.

"You poor guy! Why not join me on my party? Lots of girls and Rock n' Roll. I always had a lot of girls in my life and so…!"

Everybody created their own way of heaven here when they felt that something wasn't done right or not complete. Sam had no such desires. He had a good life. Sometimes it was challenging and frustrating, everybody has been through rough times but most of the time he thoroughly loved what he did.

Sam was now watching all the diverse people exiting the train. Friendly and helpful Souls guided everybody to the different exits. A few other People entered the train and sat down.

"Please," Sam started a conversation with a man who just had entered, "what is this city called again?"

"Oh dear man, this is no place in particular. It is a huge station fulfilling all the needs and desires that a human could have."

Sam couldn´t resist asking: "Where do you come from, now?"

"Oh, I was a doctor throughout my entire life but always had the feeling I hadn´t done enough to save the people. So I just came from a hospital where I saved hundreds and hundreds of lives and now I feel content and can move on."

The train meanwhile left the station again. Sam looked outside seeing train after train, endless tracks leading in all sorts of directions.

"Wow, I didn´t expect that this Happytrain Line Company was that big! They have a lot of trains and tracks!" he smiled at the man.

Sam´s Happytrain past beautiful landscapes, huge colorful cities and large Oceans. In fact every kind of place that one could imagine.

"So where do you get out?" the man asked Sam.

Sameena opened her eyes hearing the conductress serving a meal.

"Here, this is to get you accustomed to the food that is served at your place of destination. It certainly is not as good or real as there but here you could train yourself for your experience. By the way, there is a carriage where you could watch a film from your last experiences. This might be useful."

"Ladies and Gentleman, our next stop is "The Bridge of Flowers Station". Passengers who meanwhile have reconsidered their decision to go to their destination now have the chance to get out here and return to their families."

Sameena watched a few people getting up from their seats.

A man with a long beard looked at her: "I may be not yet ready for it!" and a woman added: "I don´t want to leave home!"

These were all good reasons and for a moment Sameena considered her decision for herself. An endless moment dissolved.

No, Sameena was a brave one, with a lot of adventurous passion in her. "I have had lives as a Sailor, a Warrior, and a Hunter. Once I was a man, once I was a woman. I was tender as a woman can be, when I was a mother and wife. I was a glorious Leader and I was an unknown poor Beggar. I was good and I was bad but I know that this time, I'm going to make it my best experience ever."

The Conductress obviously heard her saying that.

"Good and brave, so be it then. The doors will be closed now. Thank you again for travelling with the Happytrain Line!"

Sameena knew that this was the moment, when she transformed herself to a higher Being.

The train tooted a few times, as if to say Hello to his colleague train that entered the Station from the other side.

"I don't know where I will leave the train, you know." Sam answered.

"I feel pretty content inside for the moment. There is nothing that I desire especially right now, no. I will just enjoy the train ride."

He also heard two trains, tooting a warm welcome to each other.

"This is the Bridge of Flowers Station. You may reconsider your destination now. We will stay here as long as you desire."

Sam and the conductor exchanged a short eye contact and he nodded.

By coincidence Sam's carriage stopped face to face with the one that Sameena was in. They both looked outside the window and saw each other.

This was a wonderful moment of remembrance with an inner knowingness that they knew each other from lifetimes and beyond. Here they were, heading in opposite directions but their heart knew that they somehow belonged together.

"I know you!" he heard her voice inside his head.

"And I know you as well!" Sameena got the answer.

"Where have you been so long? I was waiting for you, hoping to hear from you in every moment!"

Sameena smiled, replying: "Dear one, I was with you all the time, holding your hand. I was wiping your tears from your cheek when you were sad. I was laughing in joy with you, when you were happy. What a joy it is to ceee you again!"

Time doesn´t mean anything at this Station and so endless moments in love were celebrated at this beautiful place.

They just glanced to each other, holding the other ones spirit in their heart and hands, warming their souls.

"I love you and will be with you. Know that, Sameena!"

With that the trains were set in motion again, both heading in the opposite direction.

This was not a sad moment - no Good bye with tears.

They both knew that they were deeply connected and would meet each other again. This was a plan they had both given their approval to a long time ago. They both had agreed they would assist each other with all clarity, love and compassion when it was needed.

Sam looked out of the window, seeing the train slowly passing the bridge. It was really beautiful here, a flowered doorway. He looked around and obviously there must be a different route as well because a lot of people crossed here by foot.

They all were welcomed on the other side of the bridge by old friends and this time it was an even grander celebration than Sam had noticed at the previous Stations.

Sameena also looked out of her window.

The Conductress in her cage looked at everyone explaining that there would be just one more Station before they would reach their ultimate destination.

She now felt a bit tired and closed her eyes. "I want to relax just a little…!" and then she fell asleep.

Sam also got tired. He closed his eyes, thinking about his tender but yet courageous friend Sameena.

"When will I meet her again?" and with that last thought he fell asleep.

Dreams are funny sometimes. Especially so when you are traveling on the Happytrain Line.

Here Sam and Sameena could meet and connect easily and so again they had millions of timeless times sharing endless moments. Time is irrelevant in the dreamtime.

Sameena slept when the train stopped at the so called "Near Earth Realm Station".

Some people left the train here, but they left with a purpose and seemed more to be spiritual guides or employees of the Happytrain Line rather than regular passengers.

While Sam and Sameena danced in their dream, both trains headed full speed to their last Stations.

Every train ride has a beginning and an end and so both trains entered their last Station almost in the same moment. Sam and Sameena awoke just before that happened and were both curious and excited about the things to come.

There was a last tooting, a thank you from the steam engine and a thank you for trusting in me and my work.

Sam left the train, shaking the Conductors hand who in his everlasting kindness replied by saying: "Please accept our best thanks and come back soon!"

Here he was, standing at a platform that somehow he knew from another time. His memory was slowly returning and so for a moment he tried to pursue it.

"Yes, this dog here, I know this dog!" he thought.

A dog jumped at him and was almost going crazy of expressing his joy. Dogs are like that. If you are in their heart they will always love you and circle and spin in front of you, wagging their tail like a wave of everlasting hellos.

There was not just the dog. Long beloved friends were there and friends and even more friends. It was a glorious celebration and warm welcoming for Sam.

"You are home again! Oh what a joy is that! You've got to tell us every bit of it! How was it?" and those are only a few question of hundreds that were being questioned.

We leave Sam here with his friends, you probably know where he is now. Maybe, in the meantime he will again choose to ride with the Happytrain, who knows? This only belongs to Sam and is his holy decision.

You probably now are wondering about Sameena.

Yes, she also left the train and her new adventure had just begun. She found herself in a hospital in some place on Planet Earth. She was lying in the arms of her new mom, being a little baby girl.

"We will call her Sammy!" the mom said exhausted, and her husband nodded in the beautiful presence of his wife and his newborn little daughter.

One life chapter was closed and another just begun. Sam went home to explore and decide his next steps. He would be there for Sammy, or the wonderful Angel he knows as Sameena and he would wipe her tears, cheer her on, and laugh with her as she did with him. Out of love and out of Compassion.

The Dream-Helper

You must remember this little blue Bird that helped the Mountain to fulfill his dream to ceee the Ocean.

Well, that was me.

"May I introduce myself: My name is Ohia and in your language it would mean desire or to dream of."

You probably say that we don´t exist but I can assure you, we do. We are many and we are millions and whenever you have a dream or creative thought, we would try to assist and help you.

We live in between your emotions and feelings, and we gather all the information and data that you provide when you dream. You are right assuming that we can shift in and out of physicality when it is needed, and be for example a little bird in your world. Oh, this is of course not the only shape or form we can take on. We literally can be whatever we want in order for you to take action.

In our most pure ethereal form our bodies are light blue, just that you have an idea. I know humans always need something to imagine and I am telling you this despite the fact that you never could watch us in that form. Right now we are invisible to your eyes but maybe someday will come a time when this again will happen.

It is true, most of the time we live without a body and like little ants we work day and night to try and do whatever possible to make your dreams come true.

Sadly, most of the time we get insufficient answers and information from you and today I am a spokesman to address our needs, hopes and dreams. Yes, you heard it. We also do have dreams.

I am Ohia, the Dream-Helper, but today I am here functioning as an elected spokesperson for our trade union. Yes, we have some issues to address to make our work and yours a little easier and more successful.

Let me firstly address the process of how we came to the conclusion that we should take action.

Some of my Species have huge ears. They actually can hear every little passionate reaction in your voice. To be able to do this they stick to the pathways in your throat and mouth. No need to Panic, you will never feel them!

It simply is the best place to be, to hear the words that leave you, and stating a dream with words amplifies the process. You let the world know what you are dreaming of. Be aware and pay attention to your words. They are an expression of you, an extension of your inner Being. What would you like the world to know about you?

So our buddies working in that area filter every word and if they sense something they immediately give their report to the head quarters which is coordinating the whole process.

Others of us have huge hands. They would stick to your skin and especially at your heart. Those from the Heart Section are really good at sensing the tiniest bit of excitement that would produce a stronger heartbeat. They also report to the head quarter if that is the case.

Our colleagues in your brain, as you can imagine, stick to the neural pathways of your brain. Their trademark is their always disheveled hair and partly it is because of the electrical current that always runs through their body.

They have kind of antennas to feel new connections. Also, they are similar to your computer geeks so they always analyze, write things down, calculate and so on. They are quite fun to watch!

Those three groups are connected to your body, but as I said most of us run and sense things in between your emotions and feelings.

To us it is an honor to be of service and filter every tiny reaction and the ups and downs in your feelings and emotions.

We, as you might have guessed, are very emotional as well. We have to be like that otherwise we won't be able to understand your messages.

We love to be romantic, kissing and hugging so sometimes we really need to be aware of that. Simply, we can't help it!

So, let's hypothesize and assume a buddy of ours had spotted a word that was said. He would give it to the coordinators in the head quarter. Here all the information is being collected and if there are more than three reports in a moment we start our job. It is that easy!

Now here is the problem. Sometimes we get more "maybe´s" and mutually contradictory information and we don´t know if we should start our work, or not. Then we look at each other, wondering what we should do and that´s kind of tricky.

The clearer *your feelings* are about a dream, the clearer *your statements* are about a dream, *the better* you will hear us and see our work. Together we will get closer to your dream.

Our dream is to make your dream come true, keep that in mind!

So, let's say we spotted the words, we heard your statements and the hair of our Geeks in your brain got even more disheveled because of the new connections and all the excited current that's running trough their bodies.

We love to then get into action!

A few of us have huge mouths. These little fellows actually live in your ears. They would start to whisper and cheer you on if they get the okay from their boss.

Now if there was a yes from the boss simultaneously our synchronicity group sets in. They pave the way so to speak.

Whenever a switch has to be activated or deactivated they do it. They also have the power to the muscles in your neck and so sometimes they really try hard to turn you head around, to see that dream person behind you. I belong to this group and you probably already read about my work in the Story about the Mountain and the Stone. I am always at the right place to help.

Most of the time we just do little things to assist and guide but nonetheless we do important work here and there.

The truth is that sometimes you won't listen or feel the need to turn your head, no matter how hard we try. Then others of us try to tickle you here or there. We would hide stuff from you that you then would try to find so you'd stay just a little moment longer at a certain place to find the next piece on the road to your dream.

Sometimes we would show you words on a roadside billboard but most of the time you are not aware of us talking actually to you. We use all kinds of tricks.

Haven't you never realized the 'coincidental' messages in a radio song? We are actually singing to you! Take that as a guiding system so you feel the excitement to be on the right path to your dream!

If you ignore us or you won't allow your desire to come up, it means you yourself are ignoring your own desired dream, to us this is the signal to stop. We simply go into listening mode again because all we want to do is to bring you to the highest heights and nothing less. We wouldn't want to waste energy.

So please talk to us, work with us and sense us.

To us it is simply a joy to ceee a happy fulfilled dream sparkling in glee. It is such a beautiful thing to watch and such a difference to a dream that is in a waiting mode. Oh, they are patient. Some of those dreams can sleep and wait for a long time but at one special point even the most patient dream will have enough and go seek its expression with another person. So don't take that dream of yours as a given. It comes to you to serve you and its desire is to make you as happy as you can get and even beyond.

Make it a habit every day to ask yourself if you still want that special dream to come true. This keeps our work alive and I am asking you to please trust us. We will make it work. This is our promise.

Oh, sorry I have to go!

I sensed something inside of you that needs my attention. Was there a little excitement about something?

Maybe there was a happy thought or a *what if this special thing or person would be in my life?*

Watch out! Look around. I myself will send you little messages, bits and pieces. In the end we will celebrate together. Trust me, trust it. So be it!

Wonder Dust

Wonder Dust does exist. I have felt it.

No, it is not something from a fairy tale, though story tellers often use it in their own way. It is something unique, something invisible yet so strong that it can lift a heart in an instant.

Tell me.

How would it feel if you could sprinkle it over something – Everything, especially problems would cease or simply stop existing?

Sparkle – Sparkle and the magic starts to happen.

Someone is sad? Sparkle – Sparkle, Wonder Dust, do your magic. Happiness in a blink of an eye is the promise, if it is being used.

Someone is angry? Sparkle – Sparkle, Wonder Dust, create peace inside. Yes, if you so choose, it is already being done!

I ceee love. Magic Wonder Dust, did you do this? Did you influence the lovers before they had met the first time to have a deep glance into one another's eyes and even further into their hearts? Did you do this, Wonder Dust?

Tell me your secret, share your truth. I am waiting patiently for an answer.

Dear Heart!

I AM a poem reaching around the world and up to the Stars. I AM circulating, searching, vibrating, touching hearts.

One heart? What do you believe and choose? Maybe two?

A hundred or even thousands?

Thousands of millions of hearts I engulf. I can do this.

I AM from the dusts of the Universe ...do you remember me?

I AM life expressed. Openly I say: Share me! Take me. Hug me. Embrace me and add your unique flavor to me. Add it to me and together we will create something so magical here and now, that your wildest dreams seem even to be pale compared to it. Believe me. Trust me. Come with me. Live. Be here.

Wonder Dust is the declaration of love to life itself.

Sparkle – Sparkle, let the magic begin.

I AM passionate and I AM there for you always. You just have to be available to be found.

Be present here, with a breath maybe, with attention and hunger to be alive. With love.

No need to make handstands, no need to do complicated deeds. I AM simple. I AM floating all around you in the air, flowing in the stream of a river and burning in a fire of desire.

I AM present in a hilarious joke, in a smile and dancing snowflakes from Cloud Number Nine. All this is Wonder Dust!

I AM expressed in the liveliness of a compassionate heart. I AM within the dancing creation on a piece of paper.

I AM a child singing, a bird chirping.

My essence is in a wonderful blue sky at the Ocean and it is in the playful expression in a Dolphin. I do exist.

Sparkle – Sparkle, let the magic begin.

The Wonderful Thing

"That you are in the world is a wonderful thing."

How deep and filled with love are these words. It proclaims a truth that is simple yet full of acceptance, tolerance and joy. Deep friendship is an expression of it and yes, every word in this book also. I say that to you who is reading this book, being part of a sharing world.

We now go on a time travel. We pack our bags and transcend time and space and yes, we bend physics and take a leap to meet a special friend there named Jack. We go back to visit him and the places he has been as he was young.

What? You think this is impossible?

Not for us and not in the world where we are right now, where we have ceeen talking Mountains and traveling Stones. We are going to accompany Jack, because for the adult Jack this fantasy became reality. He didn't know how or why but for some reason he could do it. He seemed to be outside of reality, like a visitor from another world.

Here he found himself as a visitor in the crimson-red barn that belonged to his father's house, where he used to play with his friends in the haystacks.

What would it be like if you as an adult could go back and ceee and meet yourself?

Jack's life back then was easy, in fact as a young boy he didn't care about problems. The only thing he was interested in was to explore the world around. He was a thinker, a sportsman and an adventurer in his own right. There simply weren't any boundaries or walls around his thoughts or ideas. It was totally different compared to the world of him as an adult, where thinking and the mind seem to rule over hearts and feelings.

Jack met his younger Self in that barn. He watched himself laughing together with his best friend Alice who was an artist in her own way.

Here in this very moment he saw himself creating a crown consisting of little daisies. He could ceee little Jack's hand picking up a flower and weaving it into the almost completed headdress.

"Ready!" he heard him saying and then he handed over the now complete crown to Alice.

"Now you are my Queen and I am your King!"

Alice put the crown on top of her head.

"No, now that I am your Queen, you must obey me!" she said and she tried to lower her young voice to sound serious. The both started laughing, running around and dancing.

"Life was so simple and joyful back then!" the old Jack thought. "How does it come that I have lost all of that?"

Yes, he knew that being an adult often means to be very mindful and cautious.

"This is a serious world where playing around, taking a break or having fun seems to almost be something like a crime. It seems that in the adult's world we always have to go and get something better, so we are valued and value ourselves. If we don't follow that road we're either judged as a loser or a lazy person. Of course this is just a mindset, something we can delete in an instant."

Who says, that it has to be like that? One, two, three and I´m going to delete it!

In that very moment Jack decided to be more joyful, even as an adult. He would go home and take time to remember how to create crowns like the one he saw.

A few moments later he found himself in a different location. Now he was a young man, trying to kiss for the first time. He could feel his heart pounding in excitement, in love but also in fear. He couldn't remember the young lady's name first but to him this wasn't important right now. It was the pure adventurous behavior of both parties that fascinated him.

He could feel the touch of hands and felt the whole universe shrinking to a tiny place inside their hearts. In this very moment time itself was witness to love.

"Love was simple back then!" Jack thought. No expectations and no "what if's" and "maybe's".

Yes, they didn't know where all this would lead to but they simply didn't care about that.

It was like jumping into a forbidden Ocean and into an unknown world, yet they both were aware of that and wanted it.

"It sounds very old fashioned in this fast forwarding world and I actually ask myself how young people feel today in those moments. Are they excited like we were back then or is a first kiss today just something that one has to do as early as possible to be cool?"

Jack´s thoughts were drifting away like waves in an Ocean of pleasure while he was watching the scene. He remembered the day and some fractions of it came back. He remembered also the name of the girl he was in love with.

In this very moment Jack decided to also change his thinking about love. "One, two and three, I decide to express my love joyful, adventurous and light. From now on, I will not just kiss in terms of the physical action. I will totally emerge in this moment of truth, for it is a holy expression between two persons and that deserves to be celebrated."

To Jack this was not a question of time and even if it were just a quick kiss to say hello, there always could be this special awareness of simple and pure love inside.

The scene faded and Jack traveled forward through his own past. Like an old video tape fast forwarding he saw his life in front of his eyes developing.

The picture stopped. He saw himself in frustration, anger and disappointment because he had just lost his job. The question that he was interested in was how he would deal with the situation, though he remembered those dark days and he already knew the outcome.

"Life sometimes is funny and at times it seems that something very important is ceasing or dying to just leave a dark abyss. I ceee this powerful illusion and relive it again in my mind. That's what had trapped me in situations, only the fear of change."

The older Jack knew that after he had lost that job he had found a new one, better paid and not only that; he met his wife exactly there. Yet, focused on the drama he couldn't ceee the positive treasures in the change.

Watching the sadness of the young man he could ceee that in his frustration his mind exaggerated the whole situation to a dark balloon that resisted every good effort of change in his mind.

"I ceee that I waited often far too long for change and I understand that either I waited till I couldn't stand a situation anymore and then broke free, or that I left others to make very important decisions for me. I was then left feeling controlled or manipulated. This all together feels like an illusion. I waited and did nothing and that, in itself is a decision as well."

Hearing that Ohia the dream-helper in the background started laughing and for the first time he felt acknowledged and visible.

In this very moment Jack decided to also change his thinking about making decisions. "One, two and three, I decide to be the Captain of my own life ship. I don't want to wait or hesitate if a situation needs adjustment and I am aware of that. I will take action.

Like an animated movie he traveled through the whole kaleidoscope of his life. He watched himself going in one direction and at times he could feel a little bit of regret and disappointment having chosen it.

"I am wondering what a tree would tell me if I would ask him if he is disappointed about how its branches decided to grow during his life. He probably would laugh and maybe wouldn't care or maybe he would say that in every single moment of his Life, life itself always chose the perfect direction. The Sun, the Wind, the Seasons and the Weather together with the tree played creation in perfection."

Maybe it is the same with our life's?

"I ceee that I regretted a lot of my decisions but I will also change that in this very moment. Like water in a river I will flow downstream in the basin of life.

If I have decided something and started to take action I will be okay with the outcome no matter what.

To me life is not just perfect when I feel okay but it is also when the result is not what I thought it would be. I simply then choose again and dive back into the streaming river of potentials."

In that moment something interesting happened.

Jack felt a tremendous relief and lightness. The first time he could ceee his new chosen potentials at work. Like a swirling rainbow he saw possibilities of his own future. He could ceee how this self healing process opened up new doorways that he never had dreamed of.

That you are in the world is a wonderful thing.

Boo!

If you would enter the dark Forest of Trust, follow the path over the Bridge of Courage that leads to the Castle of Fear you would find a little creature called Boo.

Boo was 281 years old which means he is a Youngster in terms of his career as a freaky ghost.

"You represent the fear, keep that always in your mind!" was a sentence he had heard a lot during his ghost college and to be honest he never much liked it. He himself was afraid of a lot of things and the other ghosts around him noticed that.

"You have to go see Dr. Whoo!" some said and Boo knew that this Doctor was a Ghostiologist, which translated to human terms is a Psychologist.

Although Boo didn´t feel sick he heard this statement one time too often and in the end he believed it. You see that Ghosts sometimes behave like humans and Boo felt depressed like a pancake when he called the medical practice of Doctor Whoo and scheduled an appointment.

It may be a huge laughter from the Universe and a cosmic joke but Boo had never really forgotten all the habits from his former life as a human. This in itself was pretty unusual for a ghost and Boo was wondering if he was normal.

Midnight came and with it the church bells that rang 12 times. Boo counted 9 – 10 – 11.

"12", he said aloud and entered Doctor Whoo´s rooms greeting the assistant with "Freaky Hour!" the ghost version of "Good Day!"

"And a Freaky Hour to you!" the assistance replied with a bright smile, "Doctor Whoo will be with you in a moment!"

Boo looked around and his attention was instantly caught by all the diplomas, certificates and pictures on the walls.

"Holy Ghost, this man is an expert, he even healed the Ghost of Elvis!" and he glanced at a snapshot of them both, the King of Pop playing his guitar and Doctor Whoo shaking his hips to the music.

 "Yes indeed, a great Ghost he was!"

Doctor Whoo had entered the room unnoticed by Boo who was spooked by that and winced.

"Freaky Hour, Mr. Boo! Would you please follow me and have a seat. I will see what I can do for you."

Now Boo found himself sitting on a sofa telling the Doctor almost everything he could think of about his life as a ghost.

"I am afraid of the dark and the sounds of the forest. I learned that I represent the fear itself but I am too afraid to do that. Last week when I had to scare a human, *he* almost scared me to Life. The other day when I wanted to scare a young man he tried to hug me and even to love me! Isn't that scary?"

"Hmmm yes, I mean no! YOU are in control, don't forget that!" he heard Doctor Whoo saying but his frowning forehead told a different story.

Boo went on: ''Doctor, I can hear humans talking to me.

I mean, I even hear their voices. They call it channeling and they ask me to enlighten them with my wisdom. I usually tell them to go away, or that they dialed the wrong phone number but they keep coming, asking even more questions.

I believe times are changing and being a ghost is different than it was years ago."

Doctor Whoo shook his head and he now had a worried look on his face.

"This really sounds bad, Mr. Boo. I have never had a case like this. Hearing voices and all that stuff is really a very serious issue."

"Doctor Whoo? What is Love?", Boo asked with huge eyes.

The Doc almost fell from his chair hearing that.

"NEVER say that L- Word out loud! Now I understand!"

Feeling the L-Word, thinking about it or saying it too often can cause serious problems. It is the opposite of fear and it will cause our life force to vanish into thin air.

"I will write down a prescription and you will get some medicine from the drugstore. It is the opposite of an Anti-Depressant, it helps you to get you in touch with fear again. I believe this is what you need. Don't worry, this medicine has already proved its effectiveness with a lot of my clients.

I also suggest you not to breathe deeply because this also diminishes our life force. It's better to breathe very hasty, fast and flat. This has the positive effect that you stay out of the L-Word area which causes the problem in the first place."

Boo had a bad feeling hearing that but he nodded. He was more interested in his question about Love than into taking some anti – anti – depressant medicine.

The Doctor scribbled a name on a sheet of paper and handed it over to Boo. "Here, take that three times a day and you will find your ghost life to be very fulfilling and happy. We are going to meet again in a week; have a freaky week!"

Boo was very confused. To a degree he felt misunderstood and not really himself. With tons of questions about his existence he left Doctor Whoo´s practice.

"He is a doctor, he must know.", his mind set in. "At least I should try this breathing technique."

Boo used to breathe deeply and relaxed which was also an unusual sign to his friends but now for the first time he tried it the common way and immediately didn't like it.

"I remember the sounds of the Happytrain that brought me here. When I left at the Near Earth Station waiting for my next train to the Ghost Station I could hear its snorting and tooting sound. This breathing feels like that. It is too exhausting and I don't like it!"

The short remembrance of the train brought back something that Boo had almost forgotten and this moment was an important one in his existence of Boo.

"There was a man at the Ghost Station when I left my last train. I remember hearing him say that we could come back whenever we are ready to step forward. I didn´t know what he was talking about back then but maybe I should go and find that station and go somewhere else. Maybe I will find an answer to what Love is."

The problem was that nobody knew where the Station was located. All of his Ghost friends believed that it didn't exist and even the almighty Ghost-Wide-Web this time had no clue.

"Please, I need some help! I want to step forward and don´t know how to do it. Is there anyone out there to guide me?"

His call was being heard. A small butterfly appeared in front of Boo.

"Hello Boo! I tried to reach you over and over again because I sensed that you were almost ready to move on. My name is Greta Oto but you can call me Glasswing. I will guide you to the Station and if you answer three simple questions on our way you may step into the train and depart to your next journey."

Boo glanced at the little Butterfly which was now flying in front of him. Every beat of the Glasswings left a rainbow color mark and so the whole air was sparkling.

"Follow me!"

Three Questions

Boo was happy. He had never expected something like that. So Glasswing guided Boo to the magical train station, Whether it existed or not – Boo did not know.

"The Castle of Fear!"

Boo´s fearful thoughts were loud and clear and Glasswing could read them instantly.

"What do you fear the most?"

Boo remembered his times in this Castle where he had to attend classes about fear. He learned to scare and frighten people who themselves had to play their part to be scared. It never worked out when a human suddenly behaved brave or bold when Boo tried to freak someone out and this in itself scared Boo away and made him run as fast as he could.

This experience alone made Boo cautious when he had the task to go into the human world to horrify somebody.

"You know Glasswing, one time when I scared somebody he said that he loved me. That was pretty scary to me because in my time in the Castle of Fear I was told that Love will kill my existence and I would simply vanish into nothingness. So that is what I fear the most, love or to be loved."

The Glasswing nodded his head.

"This school has taught you many things, things that they believed. You took on their beliefs like a coat and now it is time to put it down."

"I ceee that deep inside of you, you want to know what Love is and that means that you were willing to face your greatest fear over and over again. I find that pretty bold and brave!"

Boo never had heard someone calling him brave throughout his ghost life and he answered: "I never saw it like that. You mean I would exist even if I would feel love?"

"Yes dear Boo. You can leave that thought right here in that castle. You don't need that anymore especially where you are going now."

Boo and the Glasswing left the Ghost Town with the Castle and walked on the path to the Bridge of Courage.

Even if it was just a small wooden bridge crossing a small river for Boo it was like a boundary in his head.

"I can't go any further!" he suddenly said.

"Why do you think you can't move on?" the Glasswing asked. This was obviously question number two.

"I learned that I am not allowed to go over that bridge. I heard that on the other side of it are Beings that would mislead and harm me. I can't move on now."

"Boo, why do you think this bridge is called "The Bridge of Courage"?

"I don't know!" Boo replied, "I never was brave or bold unless you called me like that. I was always told that I was weak and just a Ghost."

After a short break of thinking Boo went on: "Maybe you are right. When I want to move on I have to be courageous and sometimes jump into the unknown. This time I will try."

Boo took several nice deep breaths and this time his breathing felt like he was drinking the air. In and out!

Looking from the bridge down into the river he saw a little happy stone on the ground flowing with the stream singing a song : "Let go! You have to let go. Let go! Just flow with your life...!"

The Glasswing was happy and they crossed the Bridge. At first Boo was cautious and he expected something horrible to happen any moment, but after a while Boo felt as if he had just dropped a huge and heavy weight off his shoulders. He felt much lighter than before.

With every step forward he got stronger and more lion-hearted.

"Do you ceee that this simple step over that bridge was a sign that there are actually no boundaries for you? You always had the choice to move over that inner fence - you just never believed you could do it for yourself. Do you ceee that?"

Boo was grateful.

"Thank you Glasswing, it is certainly very hard to ceee that when you are running your own movie in your head. I believe without your help I never would have come so far."

Here they were on the path to the dark Forest of Trust a place that Boo just knew from myths and hearsay.

"Boo, who do you trust the most?" this was question number three.

A moment of silence was surrounded by the listening trees of the forest. The air was fresh and for the first time Boo was able to smell. What a delight that was and Boo felt more alive than ever.

"In the Castle they taught us to trust them and to never question their statements. That was rule number one. I certainly trust you that's for sure."

The Glasswing smiled. "Thank you Boo but do you trust yourself and your inner guidance?"

Nobody of his ghostly friends ever had asked him such a question.

"I have to think about it. I seem to trust myself, otherwise I wouldn't stand here with you in this forest right? I guess I also trusted myself when stepped over the bridge and I believe I trusted myself asking constantly for Love. Yes I do trust myself."

"With that brilliant answer dear Boo, you may enter the train."

The whole scenery changed. The Forrest vanished and a train station appeared in front of Boo´s eyes. In the distance he could ceee the Happytrain standing and waiting for him, the Being that for a short moment played the aspect of a Ghost.

"Mister, Are you ready to depart?", a woman from the Happytrain Line appeared.

"I am not a Mister! I am a gh…!", but when he looked down at his body he saw that he had a human shape again wearing a nice suit.

"Welcome aboard the Happytrain! Please get a ticket at the counter and choose where you would like to go. Have a nice vacation!"

Here he was standing; he had hundreds of millions of possibilities. He smiled at the lady saying: "Thank you! I will choose wisely but for now, I guess I would just like to go home!"

The Glasswing was smiling happily.

"I am always grateful when someone finds a little bit of wonder dust! Oh, I have an appointment now and need to go! I will ceee you there!"

The Owl and the Bees

What a grand evening it was. Nice limousines brought the guests to a red carpet and the huge letters at the roof top of the cinema were lit by the flashlights of all the press people.

The "Now – Moment" was the first guest that showed up but being asked for an interview by a reporter he answered :"Sorry man, but I have no time for that!"

That´s what he always says!

 He rushed into the building in a timeless breath leaving everybody back with an open mouth.

A moment of silence followed, but then all the participants and characters in this book made their appearance. The watching crowd extended their voices cheering, laughing and yelling in an unbelievable noise.

Tinihanga with his family came, followed by Yan and Sim and Greta Oro the Glasswing.

Yan was amazed uttering something like: "Holy Butter-God!" and lovely Tinihanga made the cutest "Meeow" you could imagine. To his surprise his proud father Ika did the same for the first time and Pai hearing that fell in love with him again.

Boo the Ghost was next and he wore his Ghost costume for that special moment again, a white woven fabric. He was laughing and blowing kisses to the audience.

"Look at my new Tattoo!" he said and he extended his arm to show a red heart with the words "I love the Love!"

The Time-Zones all together came in a bus and seemingly they had already started their party on the way to this event. Miss New Zealand Mean Time was holding a glass of Champane and flirting with Mr. Moscow Time. The bus driver was the Chinese Gatekeeper who threw fortune cookies into the crowd. "May this be the best year you have ever had!"

Hop the Rabbit brought his new girlfriend, even the three Scars were happy to be here. The Stone from the mountain, the cloud and the little blue bird, Fred the mirror and Lilly the soap and all the others walked into the Cinema where the newest movie from the famous director Mr. "Luke Georgas" would soon be shown for the first time.

"The Owl and the Bees" was the title and everybody was excited.

In the last row in the dark corner there was an Italian Mafia guy, even he had shown up to watch it. It was the famous "Don Worry" who heard of the movie a while ago. "I'd like to have a tea!" he told one of his followers who instantly stood up to get it.

"Don Worry, I will bring you one!" was the answer.

Shortly before the music set in, Sam and Sameena entered the room. "We came as fast as we could, traveling with an express train of the "Yourself – Line". We are glad that we made it!" and they both sparkled in light.

The room got darker and everybody got quiet.

The Owl and the Bees was the first movie shown in 5D a new technology that allowed the audience to ceee and feel the movie by themselves on every energetic level. The "D" – note was again "d"-lighted hearing that.

The movie started.

The Owl is the all ceeeing bird in the night. With its magical eyes and ears it can observe things that others sometimes miss and fail to ceee even in broad daylight.

Pueo was a wise owl who had learned a lot during his existence, which doesn't mean he was old . After all, years in life do not make one wise alone - it is the experience and integration that makes us evolve and get wiser, to ceee that an open heart is the key to happiness.

In this story Pueo also represents the energy of the invisible and calm observer, invisible to our eyes but still very real and aware of what is going on.

Pueo was a free owl and a free spirit who enjoyed his life day after day. It is no wonder that he was attracted to a special tree where also a bee colony was living in their hive.

There were creative bees, nice bees, gentle bees and also very active worker bees. Every bee inside seem to have a special role and some work to do. Pueo observed in silence and enjoyed it.

One fine day Pueo was in the tree when he saw a grasshopper. It seemed as though the grasshopper was going through some hard times. His head lowered down to face the earth as he walked to the tree to have a little bit of a rest and a lean against the trunk.

A little bee appeared in front of him.

Free Bee was the bee with the little James Dean aspect under "his roof". He always did what he wanted to do and was the free thinker in the hive. Some of the other bees of course were seeing that and some disliked it. Being free is one of the greatest gifts in a life. It can be a great burden to feel unable to escape out of a consciousness trap, while seeing others who already have done that successfully.

Free Bee was different. When he wanted to say something he expressed it and when he wanted to go and ceee a certain place he simply packed his backpack and went there.

To reach that kind of freedom one has to let go of a lot of things and sometimes holding tight to something can shatter and shake the world and call in dramatic events.

"What's up with you?" he asked the grasshopper.

"Oh poor me. I am the poorest creature of this planet. I have no place to live and I have been through dark deep valleys in my life. In fact my life seems to be just one dark place."

"Come on, grasshopper! You can rest a bit in our home, I invite you to be our guest."

 I know that sounds pretty unusual, a grasshopper in a bee hive. Still we are in Ceee-Land where the only limit is ourselves and our imagination.

Bee Positive was the first one that welcomed them. He was smiling and his gift was to always find the good things in a bad situation. *Bee Happy* and *Bee Nice* the twins joined them, all this overwhelmed the grasshopper at first.

There was another Bee, whose name was *BC*.

Bee Ceee was the oldest bee in the hive and nobody actually knew his age. Myth says that he was over 2000 years old but there was no one who could prove that, we will just have to trust.

BC reached out his hands towards the grasshopper, shaking his hands.

"Everything in life happens for a reason. It is not that someone from the outside wants to punish you, forget that idea. No, it is you who is calling in the events for a greater purpose!"

"That is hard to believe for me", the grasshopper answered, "but you don't know my story! No one ever had a worse story than I had!"

"Yes, maybe that is true and I won't disagree if that is what you wish to believe. The only thing I would like you to question is that, this is in the past, can you change it? Wouldn't you agree that you would ceee your past differently being in a positive state? It still is the same past yet you would focus on a different aspect of it. After all, you can just can ceee a tiny bit of your past."

Bee Free added: "Of course it is your own choice on which part you want to focus. Here you are, seemingly in a bad shape. You went through tough times and no one will take that away from you. This experience is yours and you will carry it with you always – but it is just an experience."

After a short pause *BC* put his arm around the grasshopper. "Now go and have a rest in our guest room. Relax and let go of the old past. Life has a lot more to offer than suffering!"

Bee Kind guided the grasshopper to the room where a cozy bed was already prepared. The door was now closed and he was alone in the room.

"Maybe the bees were right? What If they were right and *I can change* my life just by changing my thoughts?"

A lot of questions raced through his head. He lay down on the bed, closed his eyes and after a while he fell asleep.

This night he dreamed of an owl. It felt like he was talking to a very experienced guide or a mentor and they discussed a lot.

The grasshopper had a lot of questions and the work that´s been done was truly magically. In the morning he woke up early and he felt like a huge stone was about to fall from his shoulders. He felt a bit better than yesterday.

Bee Hopeful knocked at his door. "Good morning! Time for breakfast! Come out and enjoy this beautiful day with us!"

The grasshopper opened the door. Hi Bee Hopeful, it´s nice meeting you, but what makes you think that this will be a beautiful day?"

Bee Hopeful smiled at the grasshopper. "Being hopeful is always a good state of beeing, don't you think? It needs trust at first, trusting the unknown. Expecting the good things in life will surely pull them towards you. To me it is simply a joy to ceee someone changing from being hopeless to hopeful and I invite you to at least try it."

After a second of pondering he agreed.

"I will try, I hope that you are right!"

They both went into the dining hall where all the bees from the hive were already sitting. There was a great hello when they entered the room.

"How was your night?" another bee asked. *Bee Calm* was the one with the calming influence in the hive.

"I had an interesting dream about an owl. I can't remember everything but we spoke in long terms about life."

Bee Quiet did what he always did, saying nothing and just watching. He and *Bee Calm* were very much into meditation.

His brother *Bee Passionate* started to speak:

"Right after the breakfast we will go outside to play and dance. I want to show you the beauty of nature so you can ceee for yourself! The Earth is such a beautiful place!" and his voice was almost cracking.

"I'm looking forward to it!" it was the first time that the grasshopper smiled. For the first time after his breakdown he had a good positive feeling.

Bee Good and *Bee Positive* saw the beginning change of the transformation.

Outside the sun was shining and it was a gorgeous spring day. The smell of fresh air was inviting them to go out and play.

Bee Grateful thanked the creator for all the different aspects of life, walking, swimming or flying around. *Bee Creative* had the idea to collect stones and pile them up

"In that simple way we can reconnect to Earth and cleanse our mind from those negative thoughts. Very often it is these automatic thoughts that trap us and then it is good to do something like this. After all, these are just thoughts created by our experiences and views of any given moment. If we perceive the moment or event constantly as bad and if we are not aware that we are the captain of the ship then this in the end leads to these thought patterns."

"I understand that but I have lost so many things!" the grasshopper answered. "I don't know if I can stand it or if I am able to handle that loss."

BC started to talk again.

"Losing something is a huge part in life. If you think about it then you will find out that there is actually nothing in life that you really own. Everything is just a gift that is adding something to your existence. If you lose something your life won't end. Life is endless yet we tend to believe it is not. Deep inside behind your mind you will find the feeling that simply knows that I am right."

"You may be right. But I have lost my friends. I am alone in the whole wide world!" the grasshopper replied with a sad look.

Bee Courageous and *Bee Wise* joined the conversation.

"Your never are alone and if you are kind and express love then others will come to you and be your friends. Sometimes even letting go of old friends is just a sign that you evolve or change and sometimes this is necessary. In the end it is also you who decides which step you want to take next. Some decisions are made unconscious and sometimes doing nothing about a situation is a decision as well."

"Sometimes it is hard to accept that we are responsible for our lives. It is hard to look into the mirror and accept that some decisions weren't brilliant and have lead us through more difficult roads, yet we can change it now and chose a different road in every moment."

The grasshopper listened carefully.

"I guess it is part of life, you are right. After all life is a gift and I shouldn´t waste my time on Earth being imprisoned in my mind. I will change that now once and for all."

The whole Bee colony applauded. Something magically had happened again. Life has found its way back into the Being that pretends to be a grasshopper.

The owl sat in the tree watching, listening. That is what she is always doing, you know. She is the observer behind the scene, the magical bird that ceees more that the mind can understand. Be the owl sometimes. Life is magical.

 And so it is.

"Ceee, Dear .... Your stories are far beyond being children stories, they are wonderful and heartwarming insights.... they talk of our path's and they make our inner child laugh..... I feel understood.... always your friend..... Yasmin"